POKÉMON

SINNOH HALL OF FAME

Your inside guide to the biggest and best of everything Sinnoh!

by
Katherine Fang

SCHOLASTIC INC.

New York   Toronto   London   Auckland

Sydney   Mexico City   New Delhi   Hong Kong

ISBN-13: 978-0-545-15126-9

ISBN-10: 0-545-15126-0

Published by Scholastic Inc.

SCHOLASTIC and associated logos are trademarks and/or
registered trademarks of Scholastic Inc.

12 11 10 9 8 7 6 5 4 3 2 1   9 10 11 12 13 14/0

Cover Designed by Cheung Tai

Interior Designed by Kay Petronio

Printed in the U.S.A.

First printing, September 2009

CONTENTS

Welcome to the Sinnoh Region,

a land full of new Pokémon, hidden mysteries, and top trainers! Pokémon Trainer Ash Ketchum has traveled here all the way from Kanto, and he's on a quest to challenge Sinnoh's Gym Leaders so he can compete in the Sinnoh League. Traveling with Ash are his old friends Brock, a Pokémon breeder, and Dawn, a Pokémon Coordinator from Sinnoh's own Twinleaf Town. Their Sinnoh adventures are well under way, and they've already experienced more excitement and drama than they ever imagined!

What are the moments that had the biggest impact on the three friends? Who are the unforgettable characters they've met along the way? In this book, you'll find a Sinnoh hall of fame: the top trainers, the coolest places, the most amazing Pokémon, and more! These lists are just one opinion — you don't have to take our word for it. At the end of the book, you'll have a chance to make your own list of the greatest Sinnoh moments!

But first, let's take a look at the heroes of Pokémon...

STARS OF THE SHOW

On the following pages, we'll relive unforgettable moments from Ash, Dawn, and Brock's adventures in Sinnoh. Ash has been the star of Pokémon since the beginning, but his journey would be a lot harder without his reliable friend Brock. Dawn is the new friend Ash and Brock met in Sinnoh. She's full of energy and determined to be a great Coordinator. Let's get started with a look at the moments that define who they are . . .

. . . but wait, we almost forgot Team Rocket! They may be criminals, but everyone who knows Pokémon knows all about Jessie, James, and Meowth. So turn the page for our lists of memorable moments from the adventures of Pokémon's favorite heroes — and villains!

ASH'S MEMORABLE MOMENTS

Ash's journey through Sinnoh is full of adventure, but there's more to his quest than just that! His friends know he's a talented Trainer, and he has plenty of experience and confidence in his skills. But as Ash's quest continues, he's constantly discovering new things about Pokémon and what it means to be a Trainer. Here are ten of Ash's greatest Sinnoh moments — events that shaped the hero he is today!

THE EVOLUTION SOLUTION

After Ash's rival Sho's Raichu defeats Ash's Pikachu, Ash rushes Pikachu to the Pokémon Center for emergency care. Seeing how badly Pikachu is hurt, Ash wonders if it's time for Pikachu to evolve into Raichu. Ash's greatest rival, Paul, thinks Pikachu should have evolved into Raichu a long time ago — Evolution would make Pikachu stronger! Ash decides to leave the decision up to Pikachu. He leaves a Thunderstone by its bedside  so it can choose to evolve. Turns out Pikachu is happy to be Pikachu — and that's fine with Ash!

WHEN TWO LIVES MEET

Ash and Paul are arguing over the best way to become a strong Trainer, so Champion Cynthia decides to show them an ancient inscription. The stone tablet says that when two beings meet, something new is created. What does that mean? To Cynthia, it means that meeting a new Pokémon is like meeting a new person. A Pokémon is more than a tool for battling — it's a living, breathing soul. Her philosophy lesson gives Ash (and Paul!) something big to think about.

TALKING WITH TURTWIG

Ash's new Turtwig seems to like him, so why does it ignore his battle commands? That's the question on Ash's mind after the two of them end up lost in the Bewilder Forest. As Ash looks for the way out, he takes time to share food with Turtwig and talk things over. He wants to be Turtwig's friend, and he also needs Turtwig to trust him in battle. Ash's method works like a charm: by the time they escape the forest, Turtwig is willing to listen to Ash's orders.

DON'T GO, AIPOM

Ash knows he and his Aipom are buddies, but that could all change once Jessie borrows Aipom for a Pokémon Contest. Ash can't help but spy on how Jessie and Aipom are doing. They're getting along so well, Ash worries that Aipom might like Jessie better! Even though he tries to hide his feelings, his friends know he's really upset. Ash's worst fears come true when Aipom takes off with Team Rocket. But it turns out Aipom only wanted to eat Team Rocket's fruit. Now we know how much Ash cares about his Pokémon — and vice versa!

PIKACHU'S SWEET STORY

Everybody knows Ash and Pikachu are inseparable. So what happens when a girl named Theresa asks Pikachu to pretend to be someone else's Pokémon? Ash reluctantly agrees to let Pikachu take the place of Sugar, a missing Pikachu that belongs to Theresa's aunt. Ash wants to do a good deed, but it's not long before honesty wins out and Ash tells Theresa's aunt the truth. Once Sugar returns, Pikachu returns to Ash's side — right where it belongs!

GETTING GLIGAR GOING

Ash's Gligar wants to be helpful. Unfortunately, it's no good at flying or battling! Even Ash's special training can't get it into shape. Gligar wants to evolve into Gliscor right away, thinking that Evolution will solve its confidence problem. Ash says no: he wants Gligar to overcome its fears first. After Gligar helps Ash escape a Team Rocket trap, it finally gains confidence in its own skills. Seeing that, Ash knows Gligar really *is* ready to evolve!

RAISING RAICHU

At the Pokémon Summer Academy, Ash spends two days teamed up with a Raichu. He'll be judged on how well he works with Raichu in battle, but Raichu is too shy to participate. It's even afraid of Ash! Ash struggles to make friends with his new Pokémon until he realizes that he needs to boost Raichu's confidence. Once he shows Raichu how powerful it is, the two of them put on a great battle performance!

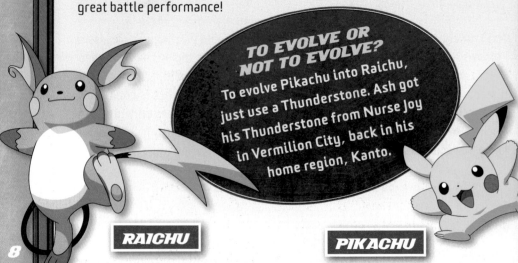

TO EVOLVE OR NOT TO EVOLVE?

To evolve Pikachu into Raichu, just use a Thunderstone. Ash got his Thunderstone from Nurse Joy in Vermilion City, back in his home region, Kanto.

RAICHU

PIKACHU

BATTLING FOR TWO

Ash and Paul are partners in the Heart-home Tag Battle Competition, and they just can't get over their dislike of each other. Ash is especially angry with Paul after seeing how Paul treats his Chim-char. When Chimchar panics during the tournament, Paul turns his back and Ash decides to call the shots for both of them. That saves their match, but Paul soon decides to abandon Chimchar for good. Of course, Ash would never turn his back on a Pokémon in need, so he invites Chimchar to join his team.

ASH'S CONTEST CAREER

Wallace, the ace Trainer and Coordinator, thinks Ash should enter a Contest with his Buizel. So Ash and Buizel compete in the Wallace Cup, and they advance to the second round. Ash's first battle opponent is Kyle, a Coordinator with a Lanturn. During their match, Buizel executes an amazing combination move that's so impressive that Ash thinks he's as good as won the match! To his surprise, Kyle is prepared for Ash's Buizel, and his Lanturn knocks Ash out of the Contest. Ash is unhappy he lost, but his friends remind him that he did pull off a great combination, and that he should be proud of his accomplishments.

THE AURA WITHIN

Ash wants to help a lost Riolu, except Riolu is wary of strangers — and that includes Ash! With a little patience and understanding, the two of them become friends. When Riolu is stolen by Pokémon Hunter J, Ash realizes that he has a special gift: he can sense Riolu's Aura. By following Riolu's Aura, Ash helps track down Riolu's kidnappers and frees Riolu for good!

DAWN'S MEMORABLE MOMENTS

Dawn is still a young Coordinator, but her travels have taught her a lot about Pokémon in a very short time! With her friends and her Piplup by her side, she's determined to take the Contest world by storm. There are still many ups and downs ahead for Dawn, but there's no doubt she'll grow up to be a winner. Let's look at ten of the major moments of her Pokémon journey so far!

TWO YOUNG WARRIORS

Dawn's travels are a good opportunity to meet up with old friends. Leona has been Dawn's friend since kindergarten, when the two of them teamed up to defeat a bully. Now Leona lives at her parents' hot springs resort, and she has her own trio of Swinub. She and Dawn join forces to stop Team Rocket from stealing all the water from the resort. Then they team up for a tag battle challenge with Ash and Brock, too!

CONTEST COMBO
Dawn's Solaceon Contest combination is called Rainbow Swift. When Ambipom spins and uses Swift, it fills the Contest auditorium with brilliant stars!

AMBIPOM

BONDING WITH BUIZEL

For trainers, catching a Pokémon is just the beginning. Each Pokémon is different and a trainer has to bring out the best in the Pokémon on their team! So when Dawn can't get Buizel to obey her orders, Lucian of the Elite Four decides to give her some valuable advice: Dawn has to adapt to her Pokémon, not the other way around! He shows her how to match Buizel's own natural timing, and soon Dawn and Buizel are battling in sync — just the way they should be!

SEEING THE LIGHT

After Dawn loses the Solaceon Contest, she's so upset that she just wants to hide in bed. Zoey knows how Dawn feels, but she forces Dawn to get back on her feet and figure out what went wrong. Zoey knows what the problem is: Dawn and Ambipom put on a beautiful show, but Contests aren't about special effects. Dawn must remember to show off her Pokémon! Dawn knows Zoey's right — she just has to turn that advice into action.

LEARNING A HARD LESSON

"No need to worry!" That's Dawn's famous phrase, and she's definitely not worried about the outcome of the Hearthome Contest's first round. So she's shocked when the judges' results are announced: she won't advance to the second round! Dawn puts on a brave face, but she can't help crying. No Coordinator likes to lose, so her friends do their best to show Dawn everyone has ups and downs.

RESCUING TEAM ROCKET

Dawn and her Pokémon are trapped in-side the Solaceon Ruins, where confused, upset Unown are all around! Team Rocket is lost in the Ruins, too, and they're on the run from the Unown. When they see Dawn, they ask her to help protect them! Dawn is reluctant at first, but she and her Pokémon still help Team Rocket until they find a way back to the normal world. Dawn may not have a lot of experience, but she knows how to keep her cool in a crisis.

GYM CHALLENGE

Gym Leader Maylene has lost the will to battle and she doesn't want to be a Gym Leader anymore. Dawn is determined to restore Maylene's fighting spirit, and she decides that honesty is the best strategy. Dawn admits that she doesn't know if she still wants to be a Coordinator, but she wants to challenge Maylene to a battle! Dawn's first Gym challenge gets Maylene back into her Gym Leader groove — and reminds Dawn how fun battles can be.

LAKE VALOR MAY-HEM

Two great Coordinators, together for the first time! May visits Ash, Brock, and Dawn at Lake Valor. When Team Rocket steals all the food from the restaurant May wants to dine at, she vows to stop them. Dawn and May take on Team Rock-et by themselves, using May's Glaceon and Dawn's Buneary to put Team Rocket on ice! As a sweet finish, May and Dawn go on to win a double battle against the restaurant's owners.

PIPLUP'S WAKE-UP CALL

Dawn hopes that entering the Wallace Cup will get her back in the Contest spirit, but she's up against tough competition. Ash, May, and Zoey are all competing, too! After Dawn sees how well they do, her fear gets the better of her and she's almost ready to call it quits. But Piplup knows better, and it hits her with a BubbleBeam to shock her back to her senses. Dawn realizes she can't give in to fear — she has to go out there and do her best!

TAKING LESSONS TO HEARTHOME

Dawn is starting to understand what it takes to be a great Coordinator, and she puts her hard-learned lessons to use in the Hearthome Collection. It's more than a fashion show, it's a chance to show off Pokémon! Before long, Dawn realizes that the fashion show isn't that different from a Pokémon Contest. The key is still to show off her Buneary, not just her dress or accessories. She designs a simple outfit for Buneary that earns her first prize.

LIKE MOTHER, UNLIKE DAUGHTER

Dawn's mother, Johanna, is a former champion Coordinator. Her mother's legacy puts Dawn under a lot of pressure. In the Celestic Contest, Dawn's biggest rival is Lila, a Coordinator who defeated Johanna twenty years ago — and wants to take on Johanna's daughter, too! Is Dawn up to the challenge? You bet! Dawn and Ambipom put on a winning performance that's sure to have a special place in Johanna's heart.

BROCK'S MEMORABLE MOMENTS

Brock isn't interested in winning Gym Badges or Contests. His mission is simple: become a top Pokémon breeder! Ash and Dawn are usually the ones in the spotlight, but their journey would be much more difficult if it weren't for Brock's cooking and advice. Here are five of Brock's most notable Sinnoh experiences so far.

BROCK'S BIG IDEA

Team Rocket steals Brock's Bonsly and a wild Nuzleaf. They also end up snatching Brock by accident! How will Brock get out of this jam? Easy: he distracts Team Rocket with his delicious cooking, which gives him time to escape with Nuzleaf and Bonsly. Brock may be a breeder, not a battler, but that doesn't mean he can't save the day.

BROCK'S EGG-CITING WIN

Brock and Croagunk enter the Pokémon Dress-Up Contest, but Brock doesn't expect to win. His Croagunk is excellent at imitating Politoed, but it's competing against Ash's Pikachu and a champion Chatot. But when Team Rocket tries to steal the prize, Croagunk stays in character even while it helps chase them down. That dedication earns Brock and Croagunk first place and a prize Pokémon Egg!

BOUNCING BABY HAPPINY

Brock's Pokémon Egg is ready to hatch, so he and his friends rush to the nearest Pokémon Center. However, Nurse Joy is afraid to help. Her Center hasn't had any visitors lately, and she's not sure she's up to the job. Once Brock restores her confidence, she helps hatch his Egg into a Happiny. As a breeder, Brock knows just how to keep his Happiny happy and healthy. That includes protecting his new Pokémon from Team Rocket's latest scheme!

MILTANK MASTER BROCK

At the Mountain Hut Maid Café, Brock comes to the aid of Autumn, a café waitress who's ready to give away her disobedient Miltank. Brock knows it's not Miltank's fault; instead, he teaches Autumn how to be friends with her Miltank, one step at a time. Both Autumn and her Miltank have trouble with the lessons, but Brock never loses his patience. Maybe he should think about becoming a teacher full-time!

CALLING DOC BROCK

Brock is away buying supplies, which means Ash and Dawn have to take care of all their Pokémon. That wouldn't be too hard, except Pachirisu comes down with a fever. Ash and Dawn do their best to cure Pachirisu, but they don't know what to do. Doc Brock to the rescue! He returns just in time to treat Pachirisu's fever and nurse it back to full health.

SHOCKINGLY SICK!
Electric-type Pokémon must keep their electricity levels balanced — they can get sick if too much electricity builds up in their bodies.

BROCK'S BIGGEST HEARTBREAKS

Brock can't help falling in love with almost every lady he sees. His dreams of romance are always crushed, but that never stops him from trying. Here are five of his biggest Sinnoh heartbreaks!

ISIS

When Brock sees a beautiful lady in peril, he runs to her rescue. He soon realizes she doesn't need a rescue after all — Isis just needs help convincing her Bibarel to cut the stone blocks needed to build a bridge. Brock and his friends are happy to lend a hand, and the bridge is finished in time. But before Brock can try to charm Isis, it's time to hit the road again.

CHERYL

Cheryl the treasure hunter is searching for the Amber Castle. For Brock, helping Cheryl with her quest is a dream come true. However, Cheryl's taken his advice to heart. She's focused on her Bug-type Pokémon and her quest for Enchanted Honey, and romance is the last thing on her mind!

SPRING AND SUMMER

Brock is charmed by Spring and Summer, two of the waitresses at the Mountain Hut Maid Café. That's why he offers to help the third waitress, Autumn, with her unruly Miltank. Although Brock hopes to impress Spring and Summer, he earns their thanks instead of their love. As for Autumn, she develops a big crush on Brock, but he doesn't even notice.

HOLLY

Holly is an experienced Trainer who specializes in Flying-type Pokémon. She's also Brock's partner in the Hearthome Tag Battle Competition. When Holly and Brock lose their tag battle against Ash and Paul, Holly leaves to keep training and become a worthy tag partner. And that leaves Brock completely heartbroken!

NURSE JOY

Everyone knows Brock adores the Officer Jennys and Nurse Joys of the world. He'll do anything to help them care for Pokémon, and he's assisted several of Sinnoh's Nurse Joys. That doesn't mean they're interested in a date, though. Because Brock has met so many Nurse Joys and had his heart broken almost every time, they're his biggest heartbreak ever!

TEAM ROCKET'S MEMORABLE MOMENTS

Okay, so the Team Rocket trio are hardly heroes like Ash and his friends. But these bumbling thieves have been part of Pokémon since the beginning, and they continue to follow Ash across Sinnoh! This book simply wouldn't be complete without a list of Team Rocket's own most memorable moments. Here are ten things Team Rocket won't soon forget about their time in Sinnoh.

RESCUING MEOWTH

Team Rocket has no problem stealing other people's Pokémon, but they won't let anyone take Meowth! Pokémon Hunter J kidnaps Meowth, hoping to sell this talking Pokémon for loads of money. Outraged, Jessie and James boldly join forces with Ash to sneak onto Hunter J's airship. While Ash searches for a stolen Gardevoir, Team Rocket searches for their missing friend. Once Meowth is safe, Team Rocket joins Ash in standing up to Pokémon Hunter J's henchmen. Just this once, there really *is* honor among thieves!

FOOLED YET AGAIN

It's the return of the Magikarp salesman! This con artist has been tricking Team Rocket and taking their money ever since they first met in Kanto. Now he's back, and he's in Sinnoh! Team Rocket aren't happy to see him, but he promises to sell them a real, working Pokémon Evolution Machine. If it doesn't work, he promises he'll give them their money back. Team Rocket really should know better by now, but old habits die hard. Once again, they fall for the salesman's scam!

AN UNDERGROUND UPSET

Team Rocket plans to tunnel under the Eterna Gym and steal its Pokémon. Imagine their surprise when they dig their way right into a mining man's tunnel! He's the Eterna City Underground Explorer, and he digs for treasure in the tunnels below Sinnoh. Team Rocket decides to help him dig in return for a share of the loot, but the Underground Explorer pockets their treasure and sneaks away! Maybe it's time for Team Rocket to get into a new business.

JESSIE'S CONTEST CAPER

Jessie has a weakness for cute Pokémon, and Aipom is one of the cutest. When she sees Ash's Aipom in trouble, she rushes to rescue it from danger! Then she borrows Aipom so she can compete in a local Contest. Thanks to Aipom's great moves, Jessie wins the Contest and a year's supply of fruit. Nice going! There's just one little problem: Team Rocket is so used to cheating and stealing, they try to steal the fruit they just won fair and square!

ELECTRIKE POTENTIAL

When James and Meowth watch Brock, Ash, and Dawn help a Trainer with his Electrike, these two thieves are so touched, they decide to help out too! A little Electrike electricity doesn't scare them one bit. Jessie tries to steal Electrike for herself, but James and Meowth actually try to stop her. Even though their good behavior doesn't last for long, it's nice to see that some members of Team Rocket have consciences after all!

MEOWTH AND CHIMCHAR'S MEETING

Ash's Chimchar is still troubled by memories of its past. After a restless night, Chimchar wakes up and goes for a walk in the moonlight. When it runs into Meowth, Chimchar is ready for trouble, but Meowth doesn't want to fight. Instead, it tells Chimchar to focus on its bright new future instead of worrying about the past. Meowth may be a member of Team Rocket, but it's still a Pokémon.

CACNEA'S NEW TRAINER

Gym Leader Gardenia is impressed when she sees James's Cacnea; she thinks Cacnea has the potential to learn the Drain Punch attack. James vows to teach Cacnea this new move, but the two of them just can't get it right. After seeing how badly Cacnea wants to succeed, James sadly gives the Pokémon to Gardenia. Gardenia will be able to unlock Cacnea's true potential, and James really does want the best for his spiky little Pokémon!

JESSIE WINS A RIBBON

Jessie finally wins a Pokémon Contest, and she does it through her own honest effort! When she enters the Solaceon Contest, Jessie is convinced James and Meowth have a secret scheme that will let her cheat her way to victory. In fact, James and Meowth don't do a thing. Jessie and Dustox defeat Kenny and Prinplup in a perfectly fair fight! Who knows how many Contests Jessie would win if she worked as hard as everyone else?

DUSTOX DEPARTS

Most of the time, Jessie acts like a diva. But behind her heartless exterior, she's hiding her own history of heartbreak. So when her Dustox falls in love with another Dustox, Jessie tells her Pokémon to follow its heart. She even crushes Dustox's Poké Ball so that it can't return!

DOUBLE TROUBLE

Jessie's Dustox evolved from her Wurmple. Wurmple can actually evolve into different Pokémon! Jessie's Wurmple evolved into Cascoon and then Dustox, but Wurmple can also evolve into Silcoon and then Beautifly.

WURMPLE

DUSTOX

CASCOON

QUEEN FOR A WEEK

When Jessie joins the Pokémon Summer Academy, she has so much fun that she forgets Team Rocket's plan to steal the Academy's Pokémon! Disguised as Jessilinda, Jessie loves all the attention she gets from the other campers on her team. Sure, they compare her to a Carvanha, but at least they look up to her! At the end of the week, her teammates tell her how much they enjoyed having her around. It's one of Jessie's best times ever!

ALL ABOUT POKÉMON

There's a reason Pokémon is called Pokémon and not Ash Ketchum. Ash may be the star of the show, but without Pikachu and its friends, there wouldn't even be a show! Let's take a look at the Pokémon who make Sinnoh such an amazing place. Who are the Pokémon to watch out for? What were the hardest Pokémon catches? Which were the most memorable Evolutions? From great Pokémon personalities to Sinnoh's extreme Pokémon, we've got 'em covered!

POKÉMON
PERSONALITIES

Every trainer has a unique personality, and so does each of their Pokémon! Every Pokémon has its own feelings and experiences that make it different from other Pokémon of its species. Pokémon battles are fun, but discovering a Pokémon's special personality is the fun part of being a trainer.

TEAM ROCKET'S MEOWTH

Is there any Pokémon in Sinnoh that's quite like Meowth? This talking Poké-mon doesn't belong to anyone — it's a full member of Team Rocket. Meowth is the brains behind their operation, and it gets stuck doing much of the work for their criminal schemes. Thanks to Team Rocket's costume collection, Meowth has plenty of practice imitating other Pokémon, but this Scratch Cat Pokémon is one of a kind!

ASH'S PIKACHU

Ash's best friend isn't a person, it's a Pokémon! Ash and Pikachu didn't always get along, but now they're a team. Ash will do whatever he can to help his buddy, and Pikachu feels the same about Ash. Brave and loyal, Pikachu also acts like a leader to Ash's Pokémon and sometimes helps interpret for him. Although Pikachu's not shy, it can be embarrassed when it's the center of attention.

PAUL'S ELECTABUZZ 3

Rude but tough, Paul's Electabuzz has a lot in common with its Trainer. As an Elekid, it would pretend to be nice to Ash's Pikachu just so it could play mean tricks. After it evolved into Electabuzz, it kept the same old attitude. Does a trainer's personality affect the way his or her Pokémon behave? Who knows? But there are signs Electabuzz's attitude may be changing: it helped Pikachu battle Team Galactic, and now it knows that not all trainers are like Paul. That doesn't mean it's turned into a softie, though!

DAWN'S BUNEARY ♀

Dawn's Buneary is as sweet and fluffy as it looks. Just like Dawn, Buneary is a young fashion fan — it enjoys browsing Poké Chic magazines along with its Trainer. However, there's one thing that Buneary truly adores: Ash's Pikachu. As for Pikachu, it's a little embarrassed by Buneary's attention, not to mention Buneary's ideas on what fashions Pikachu should wear.

ASH'S BUIZEL ♂

Even though Dawn caught Buizel, it soon became clear that Buizel was more interested in Gym battles than Contests. When it was a wild Buizel, it spent its time training and looking for battles. Because it's so competitive, it can be grouchy with its other teammates. But that intense drive makes Buizel one of the hardest workers on Ash's team.

DAWN'S AMBIPOM ♀

Ever since Ambipom was an Aipom, it's been a little mischievous. It used to follow Ash around and steal his hat for fun. Aipom is a perfect example of how each Pokémon has its own interests. It loved to show off its moves, and

Ash soon realized that Aipom was happiest when appearing in Contests. Ash traded Aipom to Dawn in exchange for Dawn's Buizel, and this performing Pokémon couldn't be happier!

DOUBLE THE FUN

Dawn's Aipom evolved shortly after learning the Double Hit move. That's the move an Aipom needs to learn if it wants to evolve into Ambipom, which has double tails!

ASH'S GLISCOR 3

Ash caught a Gligar that soon evolved into Gliscor. It was part of a lost group of Gligar, and it was always the slowest of the bunch! Gligar took a liking to Ash and happily joined his team, but Ash had his work cut out for him. Gligar really wanted to battle, but it was clumsy and bad at flying. Evolution made it more powerful, but Gliscor's personality hasn't changed one bit: it's as goofy as ever.

BROCK'S CROAGUNK 1

Croagunk has a strong bond with Brock! But who's doing the training, Brock or Croagunk? This Pokémon has an independent spirit and does what it thinks is best. It knows when Brock tries to woo pretty girls. It knows when Brock *thinks* about wooing pretty girls. And every single time, Croagunk uses a Poison Jab attack to stop Brock in his tracks!

ASH'S CHIMCHAR 5

Ash's Chimchar is one of the most intriguing Pokémon in Sinnoh. However, Paul was Chimchar's first Trainer, and he thought harsh treatment was the only way to unlock Chimchar's true power. Now that Ash is on the case, Chimchar is no longer a timid, troubled Pokémon, but it still wants to show Paul a thing or two! Thanks to Ash's kindness, Chimchar's enthusiastic personality has blossomed — although the little Fire-type still possesses more power that it knows how to control.

CHIMCHAR'S CONCERN

Back when it was a wild Pokémon, Ash's Chimchar was attacked by three Zangoose. For a long time after that, Chimchar had a terrible fear of Zangoose!

ZANGOOSE

DAWN'S PIPLUP 5

No list of Sinnoh's memorable Pokémon would be complete without Dawn's Piplup. It packs a ton of personality into a cute little package. Piplup are already known for being proud, and Dawn's Piplup is no exception. When they first met, the little Water-type Pokémon wouldn't even accept her Pokémon food when it was hungry. Now, of course, this sassy Pokémon and strong-willed Coordinator are good friends, although Piplup still gives Dawn

attitude whenever she gets too down on herself. And while Piplup is often bossy and short-tempered, it also tries to be a leader and negotiator when dealing with other Pokémon.

AMAZING EVOLUTIONS

Most Pokémon have the ability to evolve, so what makes the Evolutions below so special? When a Pokémon evolves, it's always big news for that Pokémon's trainer. Sometimes a Pokémon evolves when it's least expected, or at just the moment it's needed most. Here are some of Sinnoh's amazing Pokémon Evolutions!

BUDEW TO ROSELIA

Nando the Pokémon Bard has a Budew that's strong for its size and elegant, too! Would Budew be better in Gym battles or Contests? Nando can't decide, so he agrees to have Budew battle Ash's Pikachu. Budew evolves into Roselia during the match, but Pikachu still wins. However, Roselia goes on to help Nando win Gym battles and the Hearthome Contest!

YANMA TO YANMEGA

Team Rocket catches a Yanma for their boss, Giovanni, but Giovanni sends it back. Jessie decides to make it hers, and she couldn't be happier when it evolves into Yanmega during a fight with Ash and the other "twerps." With mighty moves like SonicBoom and AncientPower, this Yanmega could make Team Rocket a real force to be reckoned with!

MEGA YANMEGA!
Yanmega is also known as the Ogre Darner Pokémon. It's no coincidence that Jessie's Yanmega knows AncientPower — a Yanma must learn that move before it can evolve into Yanmega.

BONSLY TO SUDOWOODO

When Brock's Bonsly breaks out of a Team Rocket trap, that effort gives Bonsly the last little push it needs to evolve into Sudowoodo. Its new size and strength come in handy when Team Rocket comes chasing after Brock and his Pokémon! In its first real battle, Sudowoodo puts on a great solo performance.

DRIFLOON TO DRIFBLIM

Ash finally has a friendly battle with Fantina, the Hearthome Gym Leader. The only problem is, this practice battle is a real snooze! Fantina's Drifloon uses Hypnosis to lull Ash's Pokémon to sleep, until Ash only has Pikachu left. But Drifloon evolves into Drifblim and puts Pikachu to sleep, too. What is Ash going to do when he has to face Drifblim in a *real* Gym battle?

LUXIO TO LUXRAY

When a Pokémon evolves, it's not only its look and power that change. Sometimes the relationship between Pokémon and trainer changes, too! Marble, a young detective, has been afraid of her Luxray ever since it evolved from Luxio. Ash shows Marble that the Trainer is the problem, not the Pokémon. Once Marble starts treating Luxray like a friend, they're back in business!

ELECTRIKE TO MANECTRIC

Jaco's Electrike can't control its Electric-type moves, so it's up to Ash and his friends to help. They show Jaco how to train his Electrike. When Jessie tries to steal Electrike, it evolves into Manectric, and Jessie doesn't want to steal it now that it's grown in size. There's another bonus, too: Manectric now has great control over its Thunder attack, which it uses to wreck Jessie's Pokémon-stealing robot!

STARLY TO STARAVIA

Team Rocket have inspired a lot of Poké-mon to evolve — so they can defeat Team Rocket! When Ash's Starly frees captured Pokémon from Team Rocket's cages, it's just warming up! Starly swoops in to teach Team Rocket a lesson. It evolves into Staravia and makes sure Team Rocket blasts off for good.

CRANIDOS TO RAMPARDOS

Team Rocket has stolen a Fossil Restorer Machine from the Oreburgh Mining Museum, and they use a net to trap Gym Leader Roark's Cranidos. To their surprise, Cranidos evolves into Rampardos and breaks free of the net. Then it grabs the Fossil Restorer Machine and blasts off Team Rocket. That alone is impressive, but Roark is scheduled to battle Ash the next day — Cranidos's Evolution came at just the right time to help Roark with his Gym battles.

ELEKID TO ELECTABUZZ

Paul entered the Hearthome City Tag Battle Competition for one reason: to power up his Pokémon! It looks like his wish is granted, because Elekid evolves during Paul and Ash's final round battle against Dawn and Conway. Unlike Ash and Paul, Dawn and Conway know how to work as a team, and they have a real shot at the title. But once Elekid evolves into Electabuzz, that surge in power makes up for poor teamwork. It's the Evolution that wins a tournament for Ash and Paul!

GLIGAR TO GLISCOR

This Evolution is one that really saves Ash's hide! Gary Oak gives Ash a Razor Fang that will let Ash's Gligar evolve, but Ash doesn't want Gligar to evolve until the time is right. That time finally comes when Ash and Gligar are under attack from Team Rocket. Ash falls from Team Rocket's balloon, plunging toward the bottom of a canyon. He tosses the Razor Fang to Gligar, and it evolves just in time to save Ash. Then Gliscor uses its new-found power to defeat Team Rocket!

GLIGAR

GLISCOR

FANG TIMES FOUR
The Razor Fang evolves Gligar into Gliscor, but don't get that Evolution item confused with Ice Fang, Fire Fang, or Thunder Fang — those last three are all Pokémon attack moves that Gliscor can learn!

RISING STARS OF POKÉMON

If you asked Ash, Dawn, and Brock, they'd agree that all their Pokémon are amazing. But let's not forget all the other Pokémon our heroes have met and battled during their adventures. In that spirit, here are ten Pokémon who are truly the rising stars of Sinnoh.

FEEBAS AND MAGIKARP

Most Trainers don't associate these two Pokémon with power and might, but most Trainers aren't members of the B-Button League. B-Button League members don't believe in evolving Pokémon, so the League's leaders have trained their Feebas and Magikarp to be truly powerful Pokémon! Feebas and Magikarp defeated Team Rocket, and Magikarp defeated Dawn's Piplup and stood up to Ash's Pikachu in battle.

CHRISSY THE CROAGUNK

Chrissy belongs to the Nurse Joy in Pastoria City. She didn't enter the local Croagunk Festival, but when Team Rocket kidnapped the Festival's top Croagunk, it was Chrissy who rose to the occasion and saved the day. She took out Team Rocket's mecha Croagunk with a heart-shaped Vacuum Wave, a heroic move that earned her first place in the Festival.

FORSYTHIA'S ROSERADE 4

Forsythia is Floaroma Town's resident Poffin expert, and she has fields full of berries. Crooks like Team Rocket see those berries and think they look like an easy steal. But they haven't counted on Forsythia's Roserade! By night, it's a Pokémon hero in disguise, guarding Forsythia's fields! Forsythia taught Roserade that it's strong even without a superhero disguise, so now it's more confident than ever.

JAMES'S CACNEA

James's Cacnea loves to hug its Trainer, which is hazardous for James thanks to Cacnea's many spikes. Gym Leader 3 Gardenia saw Cacnea's true potential, and James gave her Cacnea so she could teach it the Drain Punch attack. Now that Cacnea belongs to Gardenia, anyone who challenges the Eterna Gym had better watch out for Cacnea and its new move!

COACHING CACNEA

Each Pokémon has moves that it can learn naturally through experience. But for a Cacnea, Drain Punch doesn't come naturally — it needs special coaching.

ROARK'S RAMPARDOS 4

Roark's Rampardos was originally a Cranidos. It was one of the first fossil Pokémon revived in Oreburgh City. Now that it's evolved into a Rampardos, Oreburgh Gym challengers will have an even tougher time earning the Coal Badge! Roark's Rampardos is a fast Pokémon with powerful physical attacks that can devastate its opponents.

ZOEY'S GLAMEOW

All of Zoey's Pokémon are well trained, but Glameow is one of her most dependable partners. Her Glameow has all kinds of tricks up its fur: it can use Shadow Claw in unexpected ways, or even uncurl its tail to strike an opponent! A Coordinator who wants to be the best in Sinnoh is sure to go head-to-head with Zoey and Glameow in a Contest sooner or later.

CYNTHIA'S GARCHOMP

You wouldn't expect anything but the best from a Champion, and Cynthia's Garchomp doesn't disappoint. Cynthia's battles have been shown on TV in Sinnoh, so almost everyone there has seen her Garchomp in action. It's every bit as fast and fierce as you'd expect! Cynthia's Garchomp even beat Paul's Pokémon without breaking a sweat. If Ash thinks he's going to challenge the best Trainers in Sinnoh, then he hasn't seen the last of this Pokémon.

PARADISE KINGDOM'S RIOLU

In the Paradise Kingdom, Riolu is a very important Pokémon due to its ability to sense Aura. The Paradise Kingdom always has a Riolu that serves as the Kingdom's Guardian, but the current Riolu is especially unique. It knows Aura Sphere, a move that it normally couldn't learn unless it evolves into Lucario. This ability has made Riolu a big target for Pokémon thieves, but Riolu is now safe in its kingdom thanks to Ash and Pokémon Ranger Kellyn.

COMMANDER SATURN'S TOXICROAK

Saturn's Toxicroak faced off against Brock's Croagunk when they met in Veilstone City. They didn't even battle right away; instead, they stared each other down. Once they began to battle, their showdown was cut short when Commander Saturn recalled Toxicroak to its Poké Ball and left the scene. That single encounter was all it took to turn the two Pokémon into fierce rivals! Since we haven't seen the last of Team Galactic, Toxicroak may be back for a second round — and Croagunk will be waiting.

POISONOUS POWER

Think Croagunk's Poison Jab is painful? Toxicroak secretes a poison that's incredibly potent. Just a scratch from one of its venomous claws could be very harmful!

MAYLENE'S LUCARIO

Before Maylene became a Gym Leader, she and Lucario were famous Pokémon battle partners in Veilstone City. Lucario is a Fighting-and-Steel-type Pokémon, so you would expect it to be tough. But Maylene's Lucario *really* doesn't mess around. It constantly pushes Maylene to fight and train as hard as she can, even when she thinks she doesn't want to be a Gym Leader anymore.

HARDEST CATCHES

Persistence pays off: some Pokémon seem almost impossible to catch, but trainers who hang in there are rewarded in the end. Here are five of the hardest catches we've seen so far — they may have been tough, but almost all of them have a happy ending!

DAWN'S BUNEARY

When Dawn sees a wild Buneary, she knows it would be a good Pokémon to recruit for her next Contest. It beats her Piplup, and then puts Ash on ice so it can hang out with Pikachu! But when Team Rocket captures Buneary, Pikachu must help free it before Dawn can capture it at last.

DAWN'S BUIZEL

Before Buizel was Ash's Pokémon, it was Dawn's catch — and what a catch! During a fishing trip, Dawn hooks a Buizel that manages to defeat Dawn, Zoey, and Ash before getting away. Team Rocket tries to snag it, but it has enough energy to take on Team Rocket and win. Then it demands a rematch with Piplup! Fortunately, Dawn manages to catch it. Now she has a powerful new Pokémon, and trainers can fish in the river again without worrying that Buizel will steal their fishing rods!

TYLER'S YANMA 𝒬

Tyler is a new Trainer who's been trying to catch a Yanma for days. Every time he catches up to one, it defeats his Piplup and buzzes away! Ash and his friends decide to help the new Trainer, but just when Tyler's finally about to catch a Yanma, Team Rocket grabs it and runs. Then, when Tyler tries to catch another Yanma, Team Rocket spoils things again! Only after Team Rocket is defeated can Tyler concentrate and catch his very own Yanma at last.

PAUL'S FEAROW ₃

Paul spots a Fearow in an outdoor stone maze, and he wants to catch it. Unfortunately for him, he has a lot of unwanted company. Ash, Dawn, and Brock have been separated in the maze and are searching for one another. Each of them spots Paul as he's busy with the Fearow, and they all interrupt him to ask if he's seen their friends! After the third time they interrupt his attempts to catch Fearow, Paul moves on — in the end, we never do see him capture that Pokémon. Sorry, Paul!

DAWN'S PACHIRISU 𝒬

The minute Dawn sees Pachirisu, she knows she has to have the adorable little Pokémon. It's so hyper that Dawn needs both Piplup and Buneary just to catch it. When she tries to train Pachirisu, it runs around without listening to a thing she says. Dawn sadly lets Pachirisu go. Her friends convince her to go back and get Pachirisu again, but now Jessie wants Pachirisu, too! In the end, it decides to return to Dawn, and she couldn't be happier.

DANGEROUS
POKÉMON

With a little know-how and common sense, any trainer can safely travel through Sinnoh. That doesn't mean there aren't dangers along the way: some wild Pokémon pose a special hazard to wandering trainers. It's not that these Pokémon are all mean or mischievous, but they should always be approached with care. So be cautious as we meet Sinnoh's dangerous Pokémon!

HIPPOWDON

Hippopotas

If you enter the desert where Hippowdon lives, you never know where it's going to pop up next! This huge Pokémon can easily burrow beneath the sand, so if you don't watch where you're standing, you might have an unwanted encounter with a surfacing Hippowdon! That's how Dawn's Pachirisu fell into a Hippowdon's mouth. It took a long, long chase before Dawn set her little Electric-type free again!

STANTLER 4

not Hippowdon.

Trainers in Sinnoh usually don't need to worry about being attacked by Stantler; these Pokémon aren't known for being aggressive. However, Stantler's antlers are still a big hazard! Those antlers can create powerful illusions, so it's important to be careful when looking at a Stantler. If you end up being hypnotized by its illusions, who knows when you're going to wake up?

SPIRITOMB

This Pokémon has a real mean streak. Then again, if you were sealed in a tower like Spiritomb, you might be mean, too. If its tower is damaged, Spiritomb can break free and roam the countryside, smashing anything in its way. What's Spiritomb's problem? It has a big grudge against the Aura Guardian and Pikachu who originally sealed it in the tower.

MISMAGIUS 3

Ghost-type Pokémon can be tricky to deal with — they may not always be aggressive, but some of them like to spook people! Mismagius is one example; it likes to play with lost trainers, but it has a strange idea of fun. It puts people to sleep and makes them dream that all their wishes are coming true. That wouldn't be so bad, except Mismagius wants to keep people from waking up and leaving the dream world.

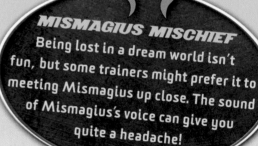

MISMAGIUS MISCHIEF
Being lost in a dream world isn't fun, but some trainers might prefer it to meeting Mismagius up close. The sound of Mismagius's voice can give you quite a headache!

ARIADOS 3

Ariados spins sticky webs that can trap anyone who wanders into its territory. Of course, a trainer can cut the web and escape, but wrecking Ariados's web is sure to make it angry. Trainers and Pokémon should be careful when they wander through the forest. Piplup and Dawn learned this the hard way!

ONIX

Onix like to live in rocky areas like underground tunnels. When Onix is upset, even sturdy Rock-type Pokémon like Golem and Graveler — get out of its way. Onix can travel at up to fifty miles per hour, so it has no trouble chasing down anyone who annoys it.

STEELIX

As with Onix, trainers have nothing to worry about if they stay out of Steelix's way. However, when Steelix gets angry, it goes on the attack, which can put innocent people and Pokémon at risk. A Pokémon this large and powerful is hard to calm down! Team Rocket learned that lesson after they accidentally hit a Steelix in the head with a shovel.

HUGE HAZARDS

Onix and Steelix are definitely two of Sinnoh's "biggest" dangers— Onix is 28' 10" tall and weighs 463 pounds! As for Steelix, it's 30' 02" and weighs a whopping 881.8 lbs!

GYARADOS

Watch where you swim in Sinnoh! Gyarados is a Pokémon who doesn't always appreciate intruders in its territory, and it's found in lakes as well as the ocean. Gyarados is every bit as fierce as it looks, with a well-known reputation for fearsome rages.

URSARING 5

Here are three good reasons not to make Ursaring mad: it's big, strong, and aggressive. On top of that, it doesn't take a lot to make Ursaring mad! Like several of the other Pokémon on this list, Ursaring has a tendency to chase anyone who crosses its path. Ash ran into an Ursaring in Bewilder Forest, and he had to battle it to protect Turtwig. It was Paul who managed to catch the Ursaring, though!

BEEDRILL 5

What's the number one hazard for traveling trainers? It has to be Beedrill. One Beedrill? No problem. A swarm of Beedrill? Big problem! These Pokémon are fast flyers that can attack with multiple stingers. They're also found in large groups and will always attack if disturbed. Bump into the wrong tree and you just might stir up some angry Beedrill. Ash and his friends have run into Beedrill swarms before, and Ash has developed a foolproof plan for dealing with them: run away!

DOUBLE THE DANGER
Here's another reason not to bug a Beedrill: its Twineedle move can hit an opponent twice, and it can be poisonous!

EXTREME POKÉMON

The Sinnoh Region is home to many unique Pokémon species, and we've gathered ten of the most extreme Pokémon for this list. These Pokémon showcase just some of the many different abilities that Pokémon possess!

EXTREME DISTANCES: MANAPHY

If you think it's a long way across Sinnoh, try making some of Manaphy's migrations! This little Pokémon can swim huge distances in order to return to the waters where it was hatched. It can even cross entire oceans! For that reason, Manaphy is also known as the Seafaring Pokémon.

WATER WARRIOR

Since Manaphy do a lot of swimming, it's a good thing that Manaphy is at home in the water. In fact, eighty percent of its body is made up of water!

EXTREMELY SPOOKY: DARKRAI

Could this be one of the spookiest Pokémon in Sinnoh? There are other Pokémon in Sinnoh known for their ghostly ways, but this Dark-type Pokémon has quite a reputation. It dwells in shadows and is known for its power to cause nightmares. So even though Darkrai doesn't mean to hurt people, there are many people who are afraid of what it can do!

EXTREMELY LARGE: DIALGA

The Legendary Dialga is seventeen feet nine inches in length, which makes it one of the largest Pokémon in Sinnoh! But it's not just Dialga's size that makes it famous. Dialga is also known for its ability to control time, and both Dialga and Palkia have been revered for their power. Although Dialga rarely appears in Sinnoh, there are statues of it all over the Region.

EXTREMELY HARD TO FIND: PALKIA

There are lots of Sinnoh Pokémon that live in extreme environments, but Palkia lives in a place where very few other Pokémon can go. You won't find it underground, underwater, or among the highest mountains: Palkia has power over space and lives in a parallel dimension! Despite all that, trainers like Cynthia still hope to see Palkia in person someday.

EXTREMELY HEAVY: GIRATINA

Giratina is a remarkable Ghost-and-Dragon-type Pokémon; it possesses two different Formes and dwells in a strange world that's linked to the normal world. It's also the heaviest Pokémon in Sinnoh! When it appears in its Altered Forme, Giratina weighs almost a ton — 1653.5 pounds, to be exact.

GREAT GIRATINA
In the Reverse World, Giratina would actually be taller than Dialga. That's because in its Origin Forme, Giratina stands 22' 08" tall!

EXTREMELY SMELLY: SKUNTANK

Some Pokémon can cause a real stink if they want to — Grimer and Muk are good examples. But without a doubt, Skuntank is one of the smelliest Pokémon in Sinnoh! It can use its tail to spray foes with a nasty-smelling liquid. Anyone who wants to bother a Skuntank should keep a distance: its spray has a range of one hundred and sixty feet!

STUNKY AND SKUNTANK

Skuntank's pre-evolved form, Stunky, also has a fearsome scent. Like Skuntank, it can hit foes with a stinky spray: in Stunky's case, the scent lasts for twenty-four hours!

STUNKY

EXTREMELY FAST: GARCHOMP

If there's a competition to see who's the fastest Pokémon in Sinnoh, Garchomp is sure to win a prize. This Pokémon is built like a jet plane and can fly just as fast, too! That's bad news for Garchomp's prey, but great news for trainers like Cynthia, who can use this Mach Pokémon's amazing speed to gain an edge in battle.

EXTREMELY COLD: FROSLASS

Sinnoh has its own snowy regions where ice-loving Pokémon can live. Froslass must be among the frostiest of them all, thanks to its icy breath. You'd better bundle up if you plan to face a Froslass, because it can breathe out a cold blast that measures almost minus sixty degrees Fahrenheit. That's ninety degrees below freezing!

FROSLASS OR GLALIE?

Froslass evolves from a female Snorunt that uses a Dawn Stone. If a Snorunt doesn't have a Dawn Stone, an Evolution is still possible: both male and female Snorunt can evolve into Glalie!

SNORUNT

GLALIE

EXTREMELY HOT: MAGMORTAR

Let's go from one of the coldest Pokémon to one of the hottest. Magmortar isn't the only Sinnoh Pokémon that thrives in hot environments, but it *is* the only Sinnoh Pokémon that uses blaster-shaped arms to shoot fireballs of over 3,600 degrees Fahrenheit.

HOT, HOTTER, HOTTEST

Magby evolves into Magmar and then into Magmortar. Even a Magby is hot, hot, hot: its body temperature can reach 1,100 degrees Fahrenheit.

MAGBY

VALUABLE POKÉMON

Who are Sinnoh's MVPs (Most Valuable Pokémon)? Every Pokémon has the potential for greatness, but there are some Pokémon who seem to be particularly popular with trainers in the Sinnoh Region, whether in their evolved or pre-evolved forms. Of course, that doesn't mean these are the only Pokémon to pursue if you're aiming for Sinnoh success. But take a look at these ten of Sinnoh's top MVPs and see who you'd like to have on your team!

BUDEW

Although Budew looks harmless, this Grass-and-Poison-type can pack a sting — and not just because of its mix of types. Its evolved forms, Roselia and Roserade, are good picks for trainers. Nando's Budew was a strong battler that evolved into a Roselia. In Floaroma Town, Forsythia's Budew eventually evolved into Roserade, the best guardian her garden could ever have! Gym Leader Gardenia has a Roserade of her own, too.

STARLY

Starly and its evolved forms can add speed and useful moves like Aerial Ace and Brave Bird to a trainer's team. It doesn't hurt that a Flying-type like Starly is also useful for scouting the area or even carrying small Pokémon! Ash caught a Starly, which is now a dependable Staravia, while Reggie has a Staraptor that knows the powerful move Brave Bird. Even Paul, the pickiest of trainers, once had a Starly.

x

45

TURTWIG

This little Pokémon can grow into something special. Turtwig isn't known for its speed, but both Ash and Gardenia have Turtwig that pack a lot of speed *and* power into a little package. Paul's own Turtwig has since become a Torterra, one of his most powerful Pokémon!

CHIMCHAR

If you need a reliable Fire-type Pokémon in Sinnoh, look no further than Chimchar and its Evolutions. It's agile and has plenty of useful attack moves. Angie met Chimchar's evolved form, Monferno, at the Pokémon Summer Academy; she saw for herself how well it does in battle. And of course, there's Ash's own Chimchar.

PIPLUP

What makes Piplup so special? This Pokémon is a hit among new trainers and coordinators: Dawn, Kenny, and Tyler all chose Piplup as their first Pokémon! Piplup has plenty of charm, as shown by Dawn's Piplup and Tyler's adorable Pippy. What's more, this Water-type Pokémon evolves into Prinplup and then Empoleon, a Water-and-Steel-type. That mix of types can come in useful!

GET OFF TO A GOOD START

In Sinnoh, every beginning trainer can choose one of these three Pokémon to be their first companion, but that's not the only reason for their popularity. Their Evolutions are also great Pokémon to have on your side in a battle, and their final Evolutions are all dual-type Pokémon.

SHINX

Need a reliable Electric-type Pokémon for a young trainer? Why not start with a Shinx! Ash's rival Angie and Landis, the son of the Pokétch Corporation president, are both proud owners of a Shinx. It has the potential to evolve into much more formidable forms like Luxio and Luxray; just ask Ace Detective Marble and her ferocious Luxray.

TURN UP THE VOLTAGE!

Every Pokémon team needs some attacking power, and Electric-types can provide a good all-around offense. They're vulnerable to Ground-type attacks, but their type gives them an advantage against Flying-types and Water-types. Perhaps that's why these three Electric-type Pokémon are popular with the trainers that Ash has encountered.

RAICHU

Ash's Pikachu gets all the attention, but this Electric-type and its Evolutions enjoy plenty of popularity in Sinnoh. Sugar the Pikachu evolved into Sugar the Raichu, and uses its moves to help roast berries for baking. Sho's Raichu and Ash's Raichu at the Pokémon Summer Academy also show off the power of Pikachu's evolved form.

ELECTIVIRE

Who says Pikachu is the only Pokémon with electric pizzazz? There's something about Electivire and its pre-evolved forms that appeals to Ash's rivals. Gary returned from Sinnoh with an Electivire that made a big impression on Ash. And of course, there's Paul and his Electabuzz. Under the right circumstances, Electabuzz can evolve into Electivire — although Paul's Electabuzz is already a difficult opponent!

DRIFLOON

The ranks of Drifloon Trainers include everyone from the renowned Gym Leader Fantina to Charlene at the famous Seven Stars Restaurant! Don't forget Marnie and Paige, two young girls who have an entire squad of Drifloon. What's so special about Drifloon? For one thing, its aerial abilities can be handy in an emergency. And when properly trained, its moves can be both powerful and versatile! Fantina taught her Drifloon to use Hypnosis and Psychic in novel ways.

LUCARIO

What makes Lucario an MVP? On its own, Lucario is a formidable Fighting-and-Steel-type Pokémon. However, it's the ability to use Aura that makes Lucario and its pre-evolved form, Riolu, so special. Don't believe us? Gym Leader Maylene and her Lucario are a famous battling duo.

WHO'S WHO IN SINNOH

Who are some of the greatest rivals in Sinnoh? Whose battles and Contests will go down in Sinnoh history? In this section, we'll take a look at all that and more, including Sinnoh's mean villains and cool characters.

TOUGH RIVALS

For trainers, friendly competition can make Pokémon battles even more exciting. Good rivals are more than just opponents: they push one another to train hard and get better! For Ash and Dawn, many of their rivals really are good friends. But while they may cheer for one another, these trainers are all business once they step onto the battlefield — and Ash and Dawn wouldn't want it any other way!

HAMILTON

Hamilton's Croagunk, Craig, won last year's Pastoria City Croagunk Festival. Hamilton fully expects to win the championship this year, but first he'll have

to beat Brock and *his* Croagunk! Brock's Croagunk faced off against Craig in the finals of the Festival, but the battle was interrupted before either Pokémon could win. Until we know which Croagunk would win in a fair fight, Hamilton is still one of Brock's toughest rivals!

SHO

Electric-type Pokémon are Sho's specialty. His goal is to collect an Evolution set: Pichu, Pikachu, and Raichu. Pikachu is the only Pokémon he still needs to find, and he has his eye on Ash's! Sho talks a big game, but his Raichu is strong enough to back up his boasts. His Raichu has one loss and one win against Pikachu, and Sho is determined to win if he meets Ash again.

LILA

They call Lila the Tiger Lily, and it's not because she's a delicate flower! Twenty years ago, Lila defeated Dawn's mother, Johanna, in a Pokémon Contest. Now she's returned to competition, hoping to defeat Dawn in the Celestic Contest! As a Poké Stylist and Coordinator, she knows how to make her Pokémon look great in battle.

ANGIE

Angie is a perfect rival for Ash: they're both generous but hot-headed Trainers who never give up! From the moment they met at the Pokémon Summer Academy, Angie and Ash have constantly tried to outdo each other. But in the true Pokémon spirit, they've also become friends who don't hesitate to help each other out. Angie might have a little less experience than Ash, since she helps out at a Pokémon Day Care instead of traveling, but she has just as much competitive spirit!

GARY OAK

Gary and Ash used to be big rivals, but Gary decided to become a Pokémon researcher instead of a top Trainer. That doesn't mean he's lost his edge, though. The two of them still have friendly battles from time to time. And although he and Ash are friends, Gary is still the bigger Pokémon expert and he doesn't mind letting Ash know it!

ASH AND GARY

Gary was in Sinnoh while Ash was busy challenging the Battle Frontier in Kanto. When the two of them met in Kanto, Ash lost a battle against Gary's new Electivire. Once Gary told Ash that Sinnoh was full of new Pokémon, it was only a matter of time before Ash had to visit Sinnoh himself!

KENNY

As kids, Kenny and Dawn were friends. Now that they're both Coordinators, they've become rivals! Kenny chose a Piplup for his starter Pokémon, just like Dawn, except his Piplup evolved into a Prinplup. He likes to tease Dawn, but he also wants to show her that he's a great Coordinator.

IT'S A SECRET!
Kenny loves to call Dawn "Dee Dee," but Dawn refuses to tell anyone where that nickname comes from. She'll get upset if you even ask her about it!

NANDO 4

Why is this Pokémon bard a double threat? He competes in Gym battles and Pokémon Contests, making him a rival to both Ash and Dawn! Most trainers would have a tough time trying to win badges and ribbons at the same time, but Nando can do both. He knows his Pokémon well and has an elegant battling style that works in any kind of battle!

MAY

May used to travel with Ash and Brock, but she decided to go to Johto and travel solo. She's honest, kind-hearted, and an experienced Contest Coordinator who gives Dawn and Zoey a run for their money. Since we last saw her, May's Eevee and Bulbasaur have evolved into Glaceon and Venusaur; together with her Blaziken and Beautifly, they form a strong Contest team!

ZOEY

Zoey is a cool, creative Coordinator who knows how to handle stress. She's one of Dawn's biggest rivals *and* greatest friends! When Dawn is feeling down, it's often Zoey who knows just what to say. And when it comes to Contests, Zoey is always ready to share her knowledge with Dawn. She demonstrates the spirit of fair play and strong competition, which makes her one of the toughest Sinnoh rivals!

PAUL

Paul may be Ash's biggest rival ever, and he's no Zoey — he couldn't care less about being *anybody*'s friend. Paul isn't even interested in being friends with his own Pokémon. The only thing that matters to Paul is power, and he'll do whatever it takes to be the toughest Trainer around. He pretends not to notice Ash, but you can bet he's paying attention. Ash wants to show Paul that strength comes from friendship between Trainers and Pokémon, yet Ash still can't find a way to defeat him!

BIG BATTLES

Contests and Gyms aren't the only place where you'll see amazing Pokémon battles. When trainers meet, the chances are good that they'll challenge each other to a friendly (or not-so-friendly) match. That's why this list features ten of Sinnoh's biggest battles, including the unforgettable fights between Ash and Paul!

ASH AND DAWN VS. BRYAN AND RYAN

What could be more exciting than a battle shown live on television? Ash and Dawn find out the spotlight's not all it's cracked up to be when their tag battle coordination turns out to be a mess! But after they apologize, they go back for another shot and this time, their teamwork wins them the match. Not bad, since they're battling the Champ Twins —who've won seventeen battles in a row before Ash and Dawn's victory!

ASH VS. ANGIE

On the second day of the Pokémon Summer Academy, all the trainers battle one another to test how well they work with a new Pokémon. It hasn't been easy, but Ash has earned his Raichu's confidence, and Angie has gotten her disobedient Monferno to trust her. So when these two rivals face off, each one is prepared for a fierce fight! The battle ends before either side wins, but Ash and Angie both show off aggressive styles that make this a great match.

ASH VS. PAUL: ROUND 1

This is the battle that sparks a huge rivalry! Paul challenges Ash to a three-on-three battle, but Ash has to decline because his Pikachu is missing. Once Ash has his Aipom, Starly, and Pikachu, he's ready to face off against Paul at Professor Rowan's lab. It's a close battle, but their final round ends in a draw. On top of that, Paul's Starly beats Ash's Starly in the first round! To Ash, this tie feels like a loss — and he's now determined to show Paul a lesson!

SHO VS. ASH

Ash has always been hotheaded, so he gets riled up when Sho suggests that he's too chicken to battle. Ash accepts Sho's challenge: it's going to be Ash's Pikachu vs. Sho's Raichu, with nothing less than Pikachu's pride on the line! Neither Pokémon is willing to budge an inch — they're both Electric-types who can match each other Iron Tail for Iron Tail. Raichu deals Pikachu a crushing defeat, but never fear: Ash and Pikachu will win the rematch.

PIKACHU VS. RAICHU

Hyper Beam is the move that really sets Sho's Raichu apart from Pikachu. Pikachu can't even learn Hyper Beam unless it evolves.

DAWN AND CONWAY VS. ASH AND PAUL

The final match of the Hearthome Tag Battle tournament is a top-tier battle: Dawn and Conway versus Ash and Paul. To make things even more exciting, Ash chooses to use the same Chimchar that Paul just abandoned! Dawn's Buizel and Conway's Heracross work together perfectly, unlike Ash and Paul. But once Paul's Elekid evolves into Electabuzz, power wins over teamwork.

ZOEY VS. JESSIE

Jessie, disguised as Jessilina the Coordinator, challenges Dawn to a double battle. Jessie is looking for easy prey and knows Dawn isn't used to double battles, but Zoey sees right through Jessie's plans. So Zoey announces that she'll battle Jessie instead! Zoey's Glameow and Shellos take on Jessie's Dustox and Seviper. Even with an injured foot, Zoey makes winning look easy; her Pokémon use Contest combinations to squash Jessie's in no time flat. While Team Rocket runs away with their egos deflated, Dawn is inspired by Zoey's example to train hard for her next Contest.

ASH VS. PAUL: ROUND 2

Ash and Paul meet again, this time in the Bewilder Forest. Paul tells Ash that his Turtwig isn't worth keeping, which makes Ash angry. Ash believes that any Pokémon can be strong if a trainer raises it right! So after they leave the forest, Ash challenges Paul to a one-on-one battle: Ash's Turtwig vs. Paul's Chimchar. Turtwig and Ash put up a great fight, but Chimchar still has the type advantage and tough moves like Dig. When Chimchar wins, Ash becomes even more obsessed with beating Paul!

PAUL VS. ASH: ROUND 3

Ash and Paul have had several great battles before, but this one is the most dramatic of them all. As usual, Ash wants to battle Paul, and Paul isn't interested. However, he changes his mind when his former Chimchar dares him to fight. The battle is short and furious: Paul's Gliscor knocks out Ash's Gligar with just one hit, and Chimchar is no match for Ursaring. That is, until Chimchar's Blaze ability takes over and sends it out of control!

CYNTHIA VS. PAUL

Although Paul hasn't even beaten the Sinnoh League yet, he decides to challenge Cynthia, the top Trainer in Sinnoh. It's a brave move, but he doesn't stand a chance. Even though Paul has a fully evolved Torterra on his team, Cynthia's Garchomp blazes right through it. It also takes down Paul's Chimchar, Weavile, and Murkrow — talk about the power of a true Champion! Paul doesn't even finish the match; he just walks away to train another day. You'd think Ash would be happy to see Paul lose, but Ash has a strong sense of fair play — and a grudging new respect for Paul.

BUIZEL VS. PIPLUP, GLAMEOW, AND PIKACHU

One Pokémon, three Trainers — and this Buizel still can't be caught! Ash and his friends hear about a Buizel who likes to steal fishing rods from trainers and then battle their Pokémon. Of course, they want to see this Buizel for themselves, and it gives them an eyeful. Buizel knocks out Dawn's Piplup with Aqua Jet, then challenges Zoey and knocks out *her* Glameow. Now it's Ash's turn! Pikachu stuns Buizel long enough for Ash to throw a Poké Ball,

but Buizel won't give up. It escapes the Poké Ball and beats Pikachu, then takes everyone's fishing rods and swims away!

MEAN VILLAINS

Even in Sinnoh, there are people who want to use Pokémon for their own selfish purposes. Fortunately, there are people who are determined to protect both Pokémon and people from these criminals and their evil schemes. Here are five of Sinnoh's meanest villains.

JESSIE, JAMES, AND MEOWTH

No matter where Team Rocket goes, they're always foiled by Ash and his friends. But what the Team Rocket trio lacks in skill, they make up for in persistence. They've been zapped by Pikachu again and again, yet they never quit trying to steal it for their boss, Giovanni. If Pikachu isn't around, they're just as happy to steal any Pokémon they can get! What could be meaner than that?

TEAM GALACTIC

Team Galactic is a large criminal organization that operates in Sinnoh. They have plenty of resources and henchmen, and they even had a giant base in Veilstone City. The police can't figure out Team Galactic's master plan, but it sounds like Team Galactic has something truly huge in mind.

PARTNERS IN CRIME?

Commander Saturn, one of Team Galactic's officers, hired Team Rocket to steal the Adamant Orb from the Eterna Historical Museum. That doesn't mean these two teams plan to join forces — Jessie, James, and Meowth can't stand Team Galactic.

GHOST GIRL 3

If this little girl asks you to play, you'd better say no. Her idea of fun is to lure Conway off a cliff and trap Ash and Angie in the spirit world. At least Jessie, James, and Meowth have a conscience that sometimes makes them do the right thing — *this* ghostly girl doesn't seem to have any conscience at all!

BUTCH AND CASSIDY 4

This Team Rocket duo is more competent than Jessie, James, and Meowth, and they're trusted with important Team Rocket missions. The two teams don't like each other, but they have one thing in common: they're always defeated by Ash and his friends. Butch and Cassidy don't normally work in Sinnoh, but Team Rocket's Professor Namba sends them to the Region so they can grab a Hippowdon for him.

POKÉMON HUNTER J

Is Pokémon Hunter J meaner than Team Galactic? Let's review. She's a mercenary with an army of goons: check. She captures and steals Pokémon to sell to the highest bidder: check. She doesn't care about the welfare of people or Pokémon: check. She doesn't even care about the welfare of her own henchmen! Pokémon Hunter J is the single most cold-blooded villain you'll find in Sinnoh. The police are on to her, but she's managed to avoid being arrested — for now.

COOL CHARACTERS

Pokémon's best characters all have certain things in common: they're not just great at what they do, they're also great because they're passionate about Pokémon. So here are the best of the best, ten of the coolest characters in Sinnoh!

CRASHER WAKE

The Pastoria Gym Leader towers over the opposition, but don't be intimidated. He may look like a pro wrestler, but his specialty isn't Fighting-types or Rock-types — it's Water-types! The truth is that Crasher Wake is a laid-back Trainer who's always ready for a good laugh. He can even be absentminded — at the Pastoria City Croagunk Festival, he accidentally left all his Poké Balls at the Gym!

ROARK

Roark is a Gym Leader as well as a foreman in the Oreburgh City mines. He has a special love for fossil Pokémon; there's nothing he loves more than looking for new fossils to study and restore. His hobby may seem a little strange to Ash, but there's no denying that it gets results. Roark's Rampardos was originally a fossil, and now it's one of his most powerful Pokémon!

GARDENIA

Gardenia is the Eterna Gym Leader and a Grass-type Pokémon fanatic. If she sees a great Grass-type Pokémon, she'll stop to admire it . . . even if she's in the middle of a battle! Gardenia also knows the Eterna Forest like the back of her hand, and she travels through Sinnoh to promote Pokémon battling. Her nonstop energy and devotion make her a cool character in our book!

LUCIAN

If you watch the news in Sinnoh, it's only a matter of time before you'll see one of Lucian's battles. He's the Psychic-type Pokémon expert in Sinnoh's Elite Four, a quartet of elite trainers. Though he's one of the trainer elite, he's no snob. Like any experienced trainer, he has a wealth of knowledge and he's happy to help Dawn learn to work her Buizel.

THE ELITE FOUR

Different Regions of the Pokémon world have their own groups of Elite Four Trainers. In Sinnoh, the Elite Four are Lucian, Aaron, Bertha, and Flint, and any trainer who wants to challenge them must first win the Sinnoh League!

REGGIE

Reggie couldn't be more different from his younger brother Paul. Paul is cold and aloof, but Reggie is warm and friendly — a true Pokémon caretaker. He looks after Paul's Pokémon while Paul is away, and he's happy to help Paul's rivals, too: Reggie even offers to teach the Brave Bird move to Ash's Staravia. He's so relaxed, you wouldn't know he's an experienced Trainer who's won badges in several different regions.

FANTINA

The Hearthome Gym Leader knows how to put on a show — maybe it's because she's a Top Coordinator as well as a Gym Leader! Ghost-type Pokémon are her specialty, and Drifloon is her special Pokémon. It's hard to find her in the Gym because she's constantly on the go, developing her own unique battling style. Inspired by the challengers at her Gym, Fantina wants to travel and train like a regular Pokémon trainer — she'll do anything to polish her skills.

MAYLENE

The Veilstone Gym Leader looks like a young girl, but she can take on almost any opponent with her martial-arts skills. She can even use her bare hands to knock Lucario's Aura Sphere out of the air! It's no surprise that Fighting-type Pokémon are her specialty, and she knows how to defend against the Fighting-type weaknesses, too. For sheer guts, Maylene gets a place on the list!

WALLACE 5

Wallace is a former Gym Leader and ace Pokémon Coordinator — is there anything he *can't* do? These days, Wallace is a big celebrity and the man behind the Wallace Cup Contest. He must be one cool Trainer: he has legions of fans who show up at the Wallace Cup wearing hats just like his! Don't think his stardom has given him an ego, though; Wallace will take time out of his schedule to give tips to young Trainers like Ash and Dawn. Famous *and* humble? Now that's cool.

KELLYN 5

Kellyn isn't just any Pokémon Ranger, he's a Top Ranger: the cream of the crop! As a Ranger, he doesn't have Pokémon of his own. Instead, he relies on wild Pokémon to help him with his missions. To recruit those Pokémon, he uses a special Vatonage Styler that he wears like a glove. Being a Ranger is cool to begin with, but Kellyn takes it to the next level. Who else could stop a runaway villain by riding a Dodrio up a cliff and leaping onto a flying Fearow?

CYNTHIA 4

Who's the highest-ranked Trainer in Sinnoh? Champion Cynthia, an elegant Trainer who's fascinated by the legends about Dialga and Palkia. One of her goals is to meet those earthshaking Pokémon in person! Like Ash, Cynthia believes that every Pokémon is a unique personality and a potential friend. But she also understands Trainers like Paul, because she was much like him when she was younger. Back in those days, all she cared about was being

a powerful Trainer. Now she's the most powerful Trainer in Sinnoh, but she's also mature and compassionate.

EXCITING
GYM CHALLENGES

Our list of top Trainers includes several Gym Leaders, and they've given their challengers some terrific Gym battles. Ash isn't the only one who's been put to the test; we've also seen Paul and Dawn battle for the badge! Which Gym challenges were the most exciting? Let's find out!

VEILSTONE GYM: ASH VS. MAYLENE

Ash's Staravia has finally mastered the Brave Bird move, and it uses it to knock out Maylene's Meditite, so Maylene switches in Lucario. In a bold move, Ash decides to have Staravia use Brave Bird again, even though it's a move that can be risky to the Pokémon using it! This time, Lucario's Metal Claw puts Staravia out of commission. Still, it's a perfect example of Ash's direct, gutsy fighting style!

PASTORIA GYM: ASH VS. CRASHER WAKE

Every good trainer knows that Water-types are weak against Grass-type attacks, so Ash thinks his Turtwig will have the advantage against Quagsire. But Crasher Wake is no fool! His Quagsire has learned Ice Beam, which is especially powerful when used against Grass-types. Ash substitutes in Buizel and has it use Aqua Jet. When Quagsire uses Ice Beam, it turns Buizel's attack into an Ice Aqua Jet combo, which knocks Quagsire out!

ETERNA GYM: TURTWIG VS. TURTWIG

Ash's 3   3 *Gardenia's*

Ash's Turtwig is faster than most Tur-
twig, but Gym Leader Gardenia's Turtwig
is just as fast. These two Turtwig battled
when Ash and Gardenia first met, so both
Trainers are eager for a rematch. Gardenia's Turtwig uses Leech Seed to sap the
strength from Ash's Turtwig, but Ash's
Turtwig uses Synthesis to recover some
of its energy. It comes down to Tackle vs.
Tackle, and Ash's Turtwig is the one left
standing!

3   3

OREBURGH GYM: AIPOM VS. CRANIDOS

Ash doesn't win this round, but it's a per-
fect example of how a Gym Leader tests
a challenger's weakness. Ash expects
Roark to save his Cranidos for last, so
Roark sends Cranidos out first to see how
Ash will respond. Ash thinks his Aipom's
jumping gives it an aerial advantage, but
Cranidos can jump just as well as Aipom!
It just goes to show that anything can
happen in a Gym battle.

ETERNA GYM:
TURTWIG & STARAVIA VS. CHERUBI

5   5   6

Ash is counting on his Turtwig's speed,
but Cherubi is even faster. That's because
Cherubi's Ability, Chlorophyll, speeds it
up when the sun is out! Time for a new
strategy: Ash is confident that Staravia's
Flying-type will give him an advantage
against Cherubi's Grass-type. But the
key to victory is the weather, not Staravia's type: Ash wins by having Staravia
attack while Cherubi is blinded by the
sun's glare.

VEILSTONE GYM: DAWN VS. MAYLENE

Dawn wants Maylene to remember the joy of battling, but Dawn doesn't plan to make this an easy fight! Even though her Pokémon don't have a type advantage against Maylene's Fighting-types, Piplup still battles as hard as it can. Lucario hits it with hard attacks like Force Palm, yet Piplup refuses to give up. Although Lucario wins, it's great to see Dawn and Piplup enjoying an exciting match.

BATTLING WITH HER HEAD

During the battle, Dawn has her Piplup use Peck, a Flying-type move. That's a smart strategy when battling Fighting-type Pokémon — Flying-type moves are super effective against them!

OREBURGH GYM: PAUL VS. ROARK

Paul's strategy is ruthless but effective: he lets Chimchar get hit by Roark's Cranidos so it can power up its Fire-type attacks with Blaze. When that isn't enough to beat Cranidos, Paul sends in Elekid and has it finish the match. The more Ash sees Paul battle, the less Ash likes him — but Paul does win the Coal Badge!

BATTLING FOR BADGES

A Gym Leader has the power to decide who receives a badge. In the past, some Gym Leaders have given out badges even when there was no Pokémon battle! So even though Ash didn't win the Veilstone Gym battle, Maylene has the authority to award him the Cobble Badge.

OREBURGH GYM: ASH VS. ROARK

Ash lost to Gym Leader Roark once, but he's determined to win the rematch. Ash knows he has to counter Roark's speedy Rampardos, and he also has a new trick he learned from Dawn. By having Pikachu and Turtwig use spins to help dodge and attack, Ash's Pokémon get an extra edge in battle! Rampardos manages to beat Pikachu, but Turtwig takes on Rampardos' Flamethrower attack and wins the Coal Badge for Ash.

VEILSTONE GYM: ASH VS. MAYLENE, PART II

The Veilstone Gym battle is a three-on-three battle, and Gym Leader Maylene's Lucario has knocked out Ash's Staravia and Chimchar! Ash is counting on Buizel, and Buizel doesn't let Ash down. It unleashes its new move, Water Pulse, and its battle with Lucario is so intense that it blasts the roof right off the Gym! The two Pokémon battle to a tie, but Buizel's fighting spirit earns Ash the Cobble Badge.

PASTORIA GYM: FLOATZEL VS. BUIZEL

Crasher Wake has a Floatzel that seems unbeatable. It can absorb just about any attack and come back for more. How does Water-type Buizel defeat its own evolved form? It comes down to Ash's creative thinking. Instead of using Water Pulse as a direct attack, Buizel uses Water Pulse to knock Floatzel down!

COOL COMBINATIONS

It's not just the moves, it's how you use them! In Sinnoh, trainers and coordinators alike work hard to come up with new combinations for battles and Contests. Here are five of the coolest combinations you'll find in Sinnoh!

THUNDER AND FLAMETHROWER

Two attacks are better than one: that's the strategy behind this battle combination! It's not a new battle tactic, but it plays a key role in the final round of the Hearthome Tag Battle Competition. Here, Paul's Electabuzz uses Thunder while Ash's Chimchar uses Flamethrower at the same time. The combination of attacks results in a mighty explosion that knocks out the opposing team, Dawn's Buizel and Conway's Heracross.

WIND AND WATER
What makes this combination especially powerful? Buizel is a Water-type Pokémon, so it's weak against Electric attacks. And Heracross is a Bug-and-Fighting-type — Bug-types are weak against Fire attacks!

WATER AND SHOCKWAVE

In the Wallace Cup, Zoey has Glameow use Shadow Claw on water to create a curtain of water around May's Beautifly. Then Glameow uses Shockwave to electrify the water! The Shockwave zaps the enemy and leaves Glameow's fur gleaming with electric power. This combination is what Contests battles are all about: making your Pokémon look great *and* defeating your opponent.

SINGING AND GRASS WHISTLE

This combination isn't used for offense, but it's still a great Contest idea. Nando has his Pokémon pool their musical abilities: Sunflora's GrassWhistle combines with Kricketune's Sing to make the music come alive. The music notes sparkle and sound waves turn into a special effect, which delights the crowd.

SINGING TO SLEEP?
The moves GrassWhistle and Sing will both put an opponent to sleep. When these moves are used in a Contest, it's a good thing the judges and the audience manage to stay awake!

FUSION OF FIRE AND WATER

Piplup's BubbleBeam and Blaziken's Fire Spin create the fusion of fire and water, a combo that turns two opposing forces into one devastating attack! May and Ash first saw the fusion of fire and water demonstrated at the Battle Dome challenge in Kanto. And now that May's shown Dawn how it's done, Dawn just might have a new trick up her sleeve!

ICE AND AQUA JET

The Ice Aqua Jet was Dawn's idea, but Ash and Buizel were the ones who perfected it. When Buizel's spinning Aqua Jet combines with an Ice-type attack, Buizel is surrounded by an icy shell that adds extra power to its attack! The result is a powerful move that looks great in Contests.

SPINNING THEIR WAY TO VICTORY
Dawn inspired Ash to add spins to his Pokémon's moves, and now both of them use spinning combinations to boost their Pokémon's attacks and dodges. Spinning combos deserve a place as one of the great ideas in Pokémon battle history!

THRILLING
CONTEST ROUNDS

A Pokémon battle is a Pokémon battle, right? Not when it's a Contest battle! It's not enough to just attack or defend; a Coordinator has to show off their Pokémon at the same time. When two top Coordinators clash, you know the battle will look spectacular no matter who wins. So sit back and prepare to be dazzled by some of Sinnoh's most thrilling Pokémon Contest rounds!

WALLACE CUP: DAWN VS. WAILMER BOY

This battle is short but sweet, a perfect example of what Contests are all about. Dawn's opponent starts the battle by having Wailmer use Brine, and Dawn's Buneary turns that attack into a chance to show off its acrobatics! Whatever her opponent tries to do, Dawn and Buneary counter it and turn it to their advantage. Even Wailmer's Surf becomes a spinning platform for Buneary!

SOLACEON CONTEST: KENNY VS. JESSIE

It's the final round of the Solaceon Contest and Kenny and Prinplup are facing Jessie and Dustox. Dawn is already out of the Contest, so she's stuck on the sidelines rooting for Kenny. He has a great Prinplup and it looks like he should be able to defeat Jessie, yet Jessie and Dustox are battling like never before. For once, she makes all the right calls and wins the Solaceon Ribbon fair and square!

FLOAROMA CONTEST: DAWN VS. JESSIE

Dawn is taking on Jessie, who's competing as Jessilina. Dawn's rival Kenny is in the audience, and she'd love to show him something to think about. Jessie goes on the attack, while Dawn has Piplup dodge to make itself look good. Piplup's Bide stores up power and then when it's ready, Dawn has Piplup hit Dustox with an attack! Jessie isn't out of it yet, but one more Peck is all it takes to defeat Dustox.

JUBILIFE CONTEST: DAWN VS. ZOEY

Dawn is excited to be battling an experienced Coordinator like Zoey. Her Buneary will take on Zoey's Glameow, and Glameow's good at turning Buneary's attacks to its advantage. Dawn comes up with a new trick herself: Buneary grabs Glameow's tail with its ears! Then it uses Ice Beam to slip Glameow up, but Zoey still wins the battle. In just five minutes, Dawn experiences her first Contest battle excitement and the disappointment of a loss.

VILLAGE FESTIVAL CONTEST: JESSIE VS. DAWN

It's not an official Contest, but Jessie really wants the Contest prize: a year's worth of fruit! She even borrows Ash's Aipom so she can compete. Dawn uses Pachirisu to battle Jessie and Aipom, hoping that Pachirisu has calmed down from its earlier case of nerves. Once the battle starts, Aipom wastes no time in showing off its great Contest moves, and Pachirisu is defeated! For Pachirisu, it's good practice. For Jessie, it's her first victory in any Contest, official or not!

FLOAROMA CONTEST: DAWN VS. KENNY

Dawn and Kenny are battling each other in the final-round of the Floaroma Contest, Piplup vs. Prinplup. If Kenny wins, it'll be his first ribbon! At first, the matchup doesn't seem to be in Dawn's favor. Kenny's Prinplup uses Metal Claw for attack and defense, and Piplup's big Whirlpool move isn't as effective against another Water-type like Prinplup. So Piplup uses the Whirlpool to change the battlefield instead. Surrounded by swirling water, Piplup battles Prinplup and wins the match!

WALLACE CUP: MAY VS. ZOEY

Both May and Zoey are great Coordinators with tons of experience, so a faceoff between May's Beautifly and Zoey's Glameow is a sight to behold. Both Coordinators make full use of the water battlefield to show off great special effects, and their Pokémon even dodge with elegance. It's great combo after great combo, finishing with a head-to-head collision over the water! When the clock runs out, May is the winner — but only by a hair.

JUBILIFE CONTEST: ZOEY VS. ASH

Zoey doesn't have much patience for people who compete in Gym battles *and* Contests. She thinks that a good Coordinator needs to concentrate on Contests alone! So when she and Glameow battle Ash and Aipom, she wouldn't mind teaching him a lesson. Aipom can use its tail to attack, but so can Glameow, and the two Pokémon battle back and forth. Ash's powerful battling style almost wins the day, but the clock runs out before he and Aipom can make a comeback! Zoey wins this round, but she admits that Ash was a worthy opponent.

WALLACE CUP: MAY VS. DAWN

This is the final-round match that has the competitors' friends and family riveted to the screen in Johto, Hoenn, and Sinnoh! May's speedy Glaceon makes its Contest debut against Dawn's Piplup, and it opens strong by using Secret Power to paralyze Piplup. The moment the paralysis wears off, Piplup takes full advantage of its spinning moves. It's a thrilling battle between two good friends, and Dawn's eventual victory gives a needed boost to her confidence!

CELESTIC CONTEST: DAWN VS. LILA

Dawn and Ambipom are going up against Lila and Delcatty, a winning team that defeated Dawn's mother twenty years ago. Lila may be friendly, but there's more on the line than just a Contest Ribbon — this is about unfinished business! Delcatty's experience is a challenge for Dawn and Ambipom, and the battle ends with a spectacular blizzard of stars created by Ambipom's Swift and Delcatty's Shockwave. When the dust settles, Dawn and Ambipom have squeaked out a victory!

MUST-SEE SINNOH

Now you've seen the people and Pokémon that make Sinnoh so amazing — but there's still more to go! What are the greatest gadgets and coolest competitions? Where are Sinnoh's top sights? This is the section that answers all your questions, starting with amazing saves that you just have to see!

BIG SAVES

In the Pokémon world, even young trainers and Pokémon have what it takes to be heroes. And since there are always crooks like Team Rocket looking to cause trouble, Sinnoh is a safer place thanks to the efforts of Ash and his friends. Here are ten of the top saves in Sinnoh!

STOP THAT STEAMBOAT!

Pikachu, Piplup, and all the other Pokémon are alone on a steamboat that's headed straight for a giant waterfall! Ash and Dawn jump on a borrowed Mantine and catch up with the boat. With Ash taking the wheel and Dawn on deck, they team up with their Pokémon to change the ship's course and steer everyone to safety just in the nick of time! Now that's one big save, thanks to teamwork — and the bravery of Ash and Dawn!

DAWN'S SOLO SAVE

Just like Ash, Dawn will do whatever it takes to protect her Pokémon. So when Team Rocket steals everyone's Pokémon and takes off in a giant flying ship, Dawn immediately leaps onto the machine to free her Pokémon. Team Rocket tosses her out in midair, but it'll take more than that to stop her. With the help of a wild Swinub, Dawn goes right back after Team Rocket and rescues the captured Pokémon!

A NOSE FOR MISCHIEF
Swinub have a highly sensitive sense of smell, which helps them forage for food. Dawn comes up with a new use for Swinub's keen nose: tracking down Team Rocket's scent!

SAVING CHIMCHAR FROM ITSELF

Ash's Chimchar has amazing power, but it always loses control whenever the full might of its fire is unleashed. That's just what happens when Chimchar battles Paul's Ursaring: Chimchar goes berserk, attacking everyone and everything! Ash knows he has to stop Chimchar before someone gets hurt, so he does the only thing he can. He runs over and grabs Chimchar as tightly as he can! Chimchar bites Ash, yet Ash refuses to let go until his friend calms down. Once again, Ash shows his stuff with a brave and fearless act.

MY FIRST SAVE

In Dawn's first adventure, she's chasing a Piplup that ran away from Professor Rowan's lab! Piplup is trapped by a swarm of angry Ariados, but Dawn's courage and quick thinking saves Piplup from the Ariados not just once, but twice! That's impressive work for a new Coordinator who doesn't even have her first Pokémon yet — all she has to rely on are her wits!

THE DOUBLE SAVE DUO

Paul's Electabuzz doesn't get along with Ash's Pikachu. But when Team Galactic's Golbat attack Electabuzz, Pikachu jumps in to protect its rival. Electabuzz returns the favor by saving Pikachu from a Golbat's sneak attack! It's a double save with a happy ending: Pikachu and Electabuzz work together to stop Team Galactic's evil plan. Not bad for two Pokémon who were fighting each other just a few days ago!

YOU'RE A STAR, STARLY

When Team Rocket uses a net trap to snag lots of Flying-type Pokémon, they also catch Ash's Starly! We've seen Ash save his Pokémon from Team Rocket before, but this time Starly isn't waiting for backup. It comes up with its own escape plan and leads its fellow Pokémon in a jailbreak! Like a true hero, Starly won't even leave Team Rocket's lair until it knows all the other Flying-types are free. For saving an entire flock of Pokémon at once, Starly definitely deserves a special mention.

PROTECTING PROBOPASS

Great trainers like Ash always put their Pokémon first. Ash's rival Alan is no exception; he'll do whatever it takes to free his Probopass from Team Rocket's mind control device! He's almost as reckless as Ash, but it all pays off. He has Dawn's Buizel and Ash's Pikachu knock both him and Probopass into lake. Once underwater, he pries off the device and restores Probopass to normal. That's one big save — don't try that at home!

CROAGUNK'S STEALTH SAVE

Brock's Croagunk is one clever Pokémon. It can even save the day without anyone knowing about it! Croagunk and Brock are watching Ash and Roark's Oreburgh Gym rematch when Croagunk senses Team Rocket's presence in the Gym. Knowing that Team Rocket is up to no good, Croagunk quietly slips away and confronts Team Rocket on its own. All Croagunk needs is a hard stare and a Poison Jab attack to make Team Rocket abandon its plan to steal the Gym's Pokémon!

ASH'S SWIFT SWIMMING SAVE

Ash never thinks twice about trying to help a Pokémon in peril. When Team Rocket takes off in a submarine after kidnapping Pikachu and Turtwig, Ash jumps in the water and swims right after them! Team Rocket's submarine dives even deeper, but Ash still hangs on. His courageous effort inspires Pikachu and Turtwig to break free of Team Rocket's trap, and Ash doesn't even mind getting zapped in the process. It's a big save by any standard, but all in a day's work for Ash!

DAWN'S DOUBLE TEAM

If an angry Aerodactyl's on the loose, what should you do? Call Dawn for a rescue! An Aerodactyl is running amok in Oreburgh City, and it's swooping in to attack Ash. Just in the nick of time, Piplup protects Ash using BubbleBeam — Dawn and her Pokémon are here to take on Aerodactyl! She's taught Piplup and Buneary new spinning tricks that make it easy for them to dodge Aerodactyl's attacks; these two Pokémon help save Ash *and* an entire city!

UNUSUAL AERODACTYL
Ash has seen an Aerodactyl before, but this ancient Rock-and-Flying-type species is a very rare sight. Unless, of course, you're one of the Pokémon researchers who have figured out a way to revive Aerodactyl using fossils!

FUNNY MOMENTS

Pokémon has so many humorous situations, it's hard to choose the top five. But here are five moments that are so funny, they're unforgettable!

PICTURE PERFECT!

Ash and Angie are always competing, but they're better at battling than homework. That leads to lots of funny moments, whether they're falling asleep in class or trying to outdo each other at drawing. Ash and Angie have to sketch Water-type Pokémon for their Pokémon Summer Academy assignment. They're feeling good about their work, but when they show each other their drawings — well, they get an A for effort, but there might be room for artistic improvement!

SWEET DREAMS, ASH!

Paul may be mean, but it's fun to see his exasperation whenever he runs into Ash. In Bewilder Forest, Ash gets lost and accidentally looks at the Stantler that roam the forest. He knows that Stantler's horns create illusions, but it's hard to avoid all the Stantler! Before he knows it, he's having a happy dream about flying alongside his Turtwig. Fortunately, Paul sees Ash swimming around on the forest floor and comes to his rescue.

COOKING MASTER ASH

Ash doesn't have a good reputation as a cook, but he's always been a confident Trainer. So even though he messed up his Poffin cooking lessons back in Floaroma Town, he decides to cook some Poffins at Mr. Backlot's mansion. Even a Swinub who eats everything won't eat Ash's cooking! Disappointed, Ash decides to try his own Poffins — and falls over when he discovers they taste just as bad as they look.

BROCK'S BIG BREAK

Brock's Croagunk uses Poison Jab on him every time he tries to charm a pretty lady. That doesn't stop Brock, but now he expects to get jabbed whenever he goes ga-ga for a girl. So when Croagunk stays behind on a steamboat while Brock and his friends shop for supplies, Brock realizes he's free, free, free! To make the most of his time, he goes crazy trying to romance all the girls in the shop. That's Brock for you!

JAMES'S REVENGE

James loves it when he gets a chance to team up with his Pokémon and enter a competition. He's sure that he and Mime Jr. could win the Pokémon Dress-Up Contest, but Jessie won't let him compete. She drags him away so he can help steal the Pokémon Egg prize. James is so sad, he mumbles his way through the Team Rocket motto. And to top it all off, he decides to give Mime Jr. a chance to shine by having it use Teeter Dance on his own teammates!

SERIOUS SCARES

Ash's Sinnoh adventures haven't all been fun and games. He and his friends have had their share of scary moments. Here are five frightening experiences that are sure to send a chill down your spine.

MISMAGIUS' DREAM WORLD

What's so scary about a world where all your dreams come true? Mismagius traps Ash and the gang in a dream world and doesn't understand why they want to leave. To keep them from escaping, it creates a fearsome purple Rayquaza. And because this Rayquaza is an illusion, Pikachu, Piplup, and Croagunk can't seem to hurt it, no matter what attacks they use. On the other hand, Rayquaza's attacks *definitely* feel real!

PIT TRAPPED!

Ash and his friends, including Marble the girl detective, are searching a mansion basement that's full of booby traps. They're looking for Team Rocket and a stolen treasure, but one wrong step could mean disaster! First Pikachu and Marble's Luxray have to dodge spiked pit traps and walls that shoot metal. Then everyone is trapped in a hallway with stone walls closing in on both sides! Luxray's acute vision manages to get them out of danger, but it's one close call after another.

A DUSKNOIR DECEPTION

Professor Rowan sends all the Pokémon Summer Academy campers on a nighttime adventure to meet Ghost-type Pokémon. But nothing goes as planned: a Dusknoir is terrifying all the campers! Conway's teammate is a ghost girl who hypnotizes him into walking off a cliff! Then the ghost girl tries to suck Ash and Angie into the Spirit World. Dusknoir turns out to be a hero — he saves Ash, Angie, and Conway in the nick of time.

SPIRITOMB VS. ASH

Ash and Dawn accidentally wreck an old stone tower during one of their practice battles. This lets Spiritomb loose, and Team Rocket convinces Spiritomb that Ash is descended from the Aura Guardian who locked Spiritomb away! Spiritomb starts chasing Ash and Pikachu — and while Ash's legs start to get tired, Spiritomb's levitation means it can chase him forever! Spiritomb nearly finishes off the exhausted duo — until Pikachu manages to stun Spiritomb with a powerful lightning blast.

HUNTER J AND THE FOREST FIRE

Pokémon Hunter J is ruthless, but who knew she was this coldhearted? To capture the Paradise Kingdom's Riolu, she orders her Salamence to set an entire forest on fire. Ash and the Riolu run away from the flames and right into Hunter J's trap! She grabs Riolu and escapes, leaving Ash to a fiery fate. Luckily, Ash's Chimchar saves him from the fire, and Ash grows more determined to stop Hunter J than ever!

GREATEST GADGETS

From classic gear to the latest in technology, we've got some of the greatest Pokémon gadgets you'll find in Sinnoh!

TEAM GALACTIC COMMUNICATOR

This handheld gadget looks like a strange whistle, but it's actually a communication device. Team Galactic may be evil, but they've got some cool technology working for them.

SPEAR KEY

Is this even a gadget? Whatever this strange box is, it transforms in the presence of certain objects like the Veilstone Meteorites. Team Galactic uses it to point the way toward the target of their master scheme, but their ultimate target is still a mystery!

TEAM ROCKET ROBOTS

Team Rocket robot technology comes at a price: paying for all these mechanical monsters has left Jessie, James, and Meowth permanently broke. There are all kinds of amazing technology in these robots and flying machines, but that technology is used for just one thing: stealing Pokémon!

POKÉ BALL

The Poké Ball is essential if a Trainer wants to catch Pokémon. It's also a safe way to transport Pokémon of any size, and it removes some of the damage that can be inflicted on a Pokémon during battle. All Trainers get Poké Balls when they first start on their journeys, but real pros look for different types of Poké Balls designed to catch specific kinds of Pokémon.

POKÉDEX

Everyone knows a Pokédex will identify the Pokémon that a trainer sees, but that's not all it does. Trainers can also use the Pokédex to analyze a Pokémon and detect what moves it can use. That doesn't matter much to Ash, but Paul always uses his Pokédex on the Pokémon he catches. He won't keep a Pokémon if it doesn't have the moves he wants!

SUPER POTION

Most trainers will recall a Pokémon to its Poké Ball and take it to a Pokémon Center if it gets hurt. But that's not always an option with wild Pokémon, so a Super Potion comes in handy for treating an injured Pokémon in the wild. Just spray it on to help heal the hurt. Of course, a trainer can use it on his or her own Pokémon, too.

POKÉMON HUNTER J'S VISOR

There's no denying that Pokémon Hunter J is completely evil, but she does have some impressive technology. Whenever she's on the hunt, she always wears this high-tech visor. Her visor works as a communicator and displays all kinds of useful data. She can even use the visor to track Pokémon that have used Teleport to get away!

CAPSULE BALLS AND SEALS

Sinnoh Coordinators like to make sure every element of their performance stands out, including their entrance. By using capsule balls and seals, they can create special effects when they release their Pokémon onstage! Seals are like stickers, except each seal has a different effect. To use a seal, stick it on a capsule ball, then put a Poké Ball inside the capsule.

VATONAGE STYLER

A Styler is a special device that Pokémon Rangers use to capture and befriend wild Pokémon. A regular Styler is a handheld device, but Top Rangers use the Vatonage Styler, which fits like a glove. Once it shoots a Capture Disc at the target Pokémon, the Top Ranger uses hand gestures to loop the Disc around the target. As soon as the target Pokémon has been captured, the Ranger can ask it for help with his or her mission.

POKÉTCH

A Pokétch is a must-have item for Sinnoh Coordinators. It's worn just like a watch, but it can be upgraded like a computer! Coordinators can pick up different applications for their Pokétch, like the Coin Toss application. That might not seem like much, but Dawn loves using it to decide who goes first in a friendly battle!

TECH POWER
The Pokétch is manufactured by the Pokétch Corporation in Jubilife City, the largest city in Sinnoh.

COOLEST
COMPETIIONS

Gym battles and local Contests aren't the only ways for Pokémon trainers to show their stuff. Sinnoh has a wide variety of competitions in which trainers can show off their Pokémon's acting skills, or even their own fashion sense! Think your Pokémon have what it takes? Then take a look at five of the coolest competitions you'll find in Sinnoh!

CROAGUNK FESTIVAL

Each family in Pastoria City raises its own Croagunk, then shows off its hard work at the annual festival! Contestants are judged on beauty as well as strength. Once a champion Croagunk is crowned, everyone puts on a Croagunk coat and dances all night long. There are even Croagunk fireworks and Croagunk-shaped pies!

HEARTHOME COLLECTION

The Hearthome Collection is a fashion show that's open to everyone. Pokémon and their owners dress up in their best outfits and strut their stuff! The winning designer has a chance to soar to the top of the Pokémon fashion world. Awards are given to the contestants with the best accessories or the most unique outfit.

POKÉ STYLISTS are Pokémon Coordinators who design fashions for Pokémon. For anyone who wants to be a great Stylist, the Hearthome Collection is a must!

POKÉMON SUMMER ACADEMY

This weeklong summer camp is a chance for young trainers to meet new friends and Pokémon. Professor Rowan holds the Summer Academy at his research facility on Mt. Coronet, where he and his staff teach classes and arrange activities to teach trainers about Pokémon. Trainers are divided into teams, and an award is given to the team that earns the most points by the end of the week. That makes the entire Summer Academy one big group competition!

WALLACE CUP

Who's the man behind the Wallace Cup? That would be Wallace himself, the champion Trainer and Coordinator. His Wallace Cup Contest is a traveling event that has been held in several different regions. If you win the Aqua Ribbon at the Wallace Cup, it counts as a Contest win in any region! So when the Wallace Cup comes to Sinnoh's own Lake Valor, May returns from Johto to compete alongside Dawn and Zoey. It's more than a Contest, it's a Coordinator reunion!

POKÉMON DRESS-UP CONTEST

Ash has a great Pikachu, but does it make a great Wobbuffet? Or a Mudkip? In the Pokémon Dress-Up Contest, trainers compete to see whose Pokémon is best at imitating other Pokémon! Costumes are allowed, but Pokémon lose points if they don't stay in character.

The Dress-Up Contest's lucky winner receives a Pokémon Egg as a prize. This competition is definitely one of the most creative contests in Sinnoh.

DRESSING FOR SUCCESS

The Pokémon Dress-Up Contest was created by the Pokémon Fan Club, and it's number one in the Sinnoh TV ratings!

SECRET
SIGHTS

Sinnoh is home to many wonderful sights, but many of them can only be seen if you know exactly where to look! Most Trainers would be lucky to see even one of these hidden surprises, but we've got ten of Sinnoh's best secret sights right here!

MATTHEW'S MANSION

Matthew is a pleasant, wealthy old man with a mansion so big, it's impossible to miss! So what's secret about his house? The secret is hidden beneath the mansion: the basement is a maze of passages and vicious booby traps. Visitors who take one wrong step in his house could end up lost in a deadly dungeon that's straight out of an action movie!

SHIELDON SANCTUARY

Somewhere near Mt. Coronet, there's a wild, unspoiled area where Shieldon live. The exact coordinates aren't public knowledge, because these rare Pokémon are being studied and protected by Gary and Professor Rowan. Gary hopes to turn the area into a nature preserve, so perhaps visitors can come see Shieldon themselves someday.

A PREHISTORIC POKÉMON
Shieldon may be rare, but they've been around for millions of years. Ancient jungles were their original habitat.

DUSTOX CROSSING

Some of Sinnoh's greatest sights are hard to find because they only last for a few hours! In the mountains of Sinnoh, there's a serene lake where a special event happens for just one night out of each year. On that night, the moonlight reflected off the lake attracts Dustox and causes them to make the Dustox Crossing. During the Crossing, Dustox will pair up with a mate and fly off over Mt. Coronet. As they fly, they leave a glittering golden trail in the night sky.

BIDOOF VILLAGE

Trainers meet lots of Pokémon on their journeys, but how often does a trainer see how Pokémon truly live in the wild? Ash and his friends stumble upon a Bidoof village while trying to help a lost Bidoof. This large Bidoof community is safely hidden behind rocky walls, and the Bidoof have built many round, leafy nests. These remarkable homes are big enough for more than one Bidoof — or an entire Team Rocket trio.

AT HOME IN THE WATER
Bidoof like to make their nests near the water. That's why this Bidoof village is located near a waterfall!

THE SUNKEN TOWN

Travelers on the way to Hearthome City may pass a peaceful lake that lies just behind a dam. The lake hides an unusual secret: before the dam was built, this area was actually a town! The citizens had to leave when the dam was built, but their entire town is still there, preserved beneath the water. Anyone who takes a scenic dive needs to watch out for one thing first, though: the local Gyarados!

The Summit Ruins are at the top of a wooded hill that's near Professor Rowan's Mt. Coronet facility. Professor Rowan and his team are renovating the ruins, and there's a cave beneath the ruins that might be the entrance to the spirit world. A Dusknoir sealed up the cavern entrance, so who knows for sure what's hiding down there? That's one secret nobody is eager to explore!

SOLACEON RUINS

Anyone can go visit the Solaceon Ruins near Solaceon Town; trainers can even battle in the shadow of its towering statues of Dialga and Palkia. Inside the ruins, though, there are stone chambers filled with strange carvings. When the carvings are activated with special plates, the Ruins transform and come alive with Unown! Anyone in the area will be trapped inside, lost in a realm where the dimensions have been flipped upside down.

SUICUNE'S LAKE

Trainers may be lucky enough to spot Suicune if they know where to look in the forest near the Valley Windworks Power Plant. In those woods, there's a hidden lake where Suicune can often be found. Even for an experienced trainer, seeing Suicune is a rare opportunity — but this Legendary Pokémon regularly plays with the daughters of the local Nurse Joy!

WIND AND WATER
Suicune is known as the spirit of the North Wind, but it does have a connection to water: it's known for purifying water wherever it goes.

THE THREE LAKES

Lake Verity, Lake Valor, and Lake Acuity are all linked by a certain legend. It's said that there are Pokémon beneath these three lakes, but they're almost never seen. However, Dawn saw something floating over Lake Verity, and Ash saw a similar creature floating over Lake Valor. There's clearly something going on, and whoever sees those rare Pokémon will be one step closer to understanding the Sinnoh space-time legends.

THE AMBER CASTLE

Somewhere in Eterna Forest lies the Amber Castle, a hive full of Combee and their Vespiquen that holds the super-sweet Enchanted Honey. To find it, treasure hunters must search for Combee Walls, clusters of Combee that occur near the Amber Castle. That's not all, because Amber Castle itself lies deep inside a cave whose entrance is hidden by a waterfall. But thieves beware, because the Castle is guarded by swarms of Combee!

SWEET AS CAN BEEDRILL

Honey can be used attract wild Pokémon. Because the Enchanted Honey is many times sweeter than normal honey, it can be a powerful Pokémon lure!

AMAZING ATTRACTIONS

Here are the places that any trainer can visit, and everyone should see: Sinnoh's most amazing attractions!

MR. BACKLOT'S TROPHY GARDEN

Mr. Backlot loves Pokémon, so he's turned the land around his mansion into a Trophy Garden where his Pokémon can roam. Thanks to Mr. Backlot's generous nature, Pokémon breeders, Watchers, and trainers are all welcome to visit the Trophy Garden and observe the Pokémon. Since Mr. Backlot is hospitable as well, he doesn't seem to mind letting visitors stay in his mansion. Among the Pokémon that trainers might see are Mr. Backlot's Cleffa, Pichu, and Azurill!

FLOAROMA TOWN

According to old stories, the area around Floaroma Town used to be a barren land. It wasn't until people gave thanks to nature that the earth blossomed, and now Floaroma Town is known as the town of vivid and scented flowers. The Floaroma Contest is a big destination for Coordinators, but all visitors can enjoy visiting the town. It's like one big flower garden!

ETERNA HISTORICAL MUSEUM

Most people imagine a museum as a place full of paintings and sculptures. But what if a museum held a key to an ancient mystery? That's the case at the Eterna Historical Museum, where the Adamant Orb is on display. Researchers believe that this relic can make Dialga more powerful, so anyone interested in Sinnoh's space-time legends can't miss a chance to visit the museum. Just don't touch the exhibits, because Officer Jenny takes the museum's security very seriously!

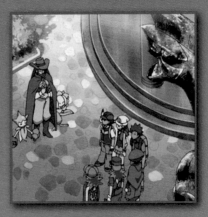

VEILSTONE CITY METEORITES

Veilstone City is famous for its field of meteorites; local legend even says that these rocks are the city's guardians. Nobody knows how these glowing meteorites ended up in the field, but Veilstone City developed as more and more people came to see the sight. Team Galactic seems to think there really is something special about those meteorites — that's why they want to steal them.

OREBURGH MINING MUSEUM

History literally comes alive at the Oreburgh Mining Museum! There's much more to see here than exhibits about the history of minerals. Half of the museum is a research facility that houses a special Fossil Restorer Machine — scientists here bring Pokémon fossils back to life! The revived Pokémon are kept in the research wing, where they can live in environments that recreate the ancient world.

UNIQUE STYLES

We're not done yet! Here's one more must-see: Sinnoh's most unique styles!

CRASHER WAKE COSTUME

Is there anyone in Sinnoh who's brave enough to wear a white shirt over a colorful wrestler's outfit? There's only one man in Sinnoh who fits that description, and he's Crasher Wake!

MAY'S WALLACE CUP OUTFIT

May's Wallace Cup costume makes her look like a princess on the stage!

ASH'S HEARTHOME COLLECTION OUTFIT

Ash and Pikachu enter the Hearthome Collection fashion contest, but Ash doesn't know how to sew. That's okay — Brock comes up with a memorable costume for the pair to wear. It's not exactly high fashion, but it does earn Ash and Pikachu an award for having the most unique outfits.

TEAM ROCKET

Team Rocket likes to make fun of Team Galactic's fashion sense, and Jessie, James, and Meowth definitely know something about clothes. Dressing up is the one thing they're good at — they have outfits for every occasion! If there was a Sinnoh lifetime award for unique style, Team Rocket would win it for their costume collection.